UNSCRUPULOUS

Wanted

MORGAN LEE WYLIE

Sisu Publishing | Kuna, Idaho | First Edition, 2020
Print ISBN: 978-1-7324853-2-7
eBook ISBN: 978-1-7324853-3-4

Library of Congress Control Number: 2020921037

Book cover design by www.ebooklaunch.com
Golden Whiskey licensed from OlegVoznyy

Published in the United States of America

For the readers who asked for more,
This book would not exist if not for you.

1

The jailhouse was empty, the sheriff its only inmate. Trace Malloy sat on the edge of a hard cot with his boots planted wide, hand on one knee, elbow on the other. He unpinned the star from his vest and held it in the faint light afforded by a high, barred window. He massaged the surface with his thumb, bringing a shine to the nickel. In his thoughts, a voice from the past echoed its unheeded counsel. *You will not be rewarded for taking up this charge.*

Two years ago, Trace came home to Arizona Territory too late to bury his parents, too late to protect his sister, too late to prevent too much injustice. He vowed to bring retribution to the devils responsible, to expel the corruption that gave lawlessness free rein. Two years ago, he became sheriff.

He looked around at what he had to show for it, a one-cell jailhouse in Prospect, the county seat. He had a desk with a typewriter for making reports, a safe for locking up ammunition and firearms, and a bulletin upon which maps, notices, and wanted posters were periodically swapped for updated versions. There was a cot inside the cell for prisoners and one outside it for nights Trace didn't feel like returning to the rowdy boarding house where he kept a room. Books inherited from his mentor sat on a shelf collecting dust. Neither had prepared him for the reality of his sworn duty, though ranger-turned-judge Del Cooper had tried to impart some of that wisdom which only experience brings, warning Trace of the sacrifice incumbent upon a lawman. *He starts with his principles and integrity, and in the end, they are all he can expect to keep.*

A fart roused him from his brown study, courtesy of the spotted hound that lay sprawled out, drooling on the wood floor. Trace groaned and pushed to his feet, stepping over the dog to open the door. A cross-breeze began to circulate hot, seasonally humid air through the small building. The hound scrambled to its paws, at its master's heels, only to collapse upon the shaded boardwalk planks, back into slumber, when it realized he was going no further. Trace propped his shoulder against the doorframe and squinted against the glare of the sun, surveying the current of frontier life flowing past his vantage point.

The country marched toward the turn of the century, but where invention and industry advanced the more populated towns, sparser western settlements still wrought a rough existence. The roads were unpaved, the traffic horse-and-cart. The telephone had yet to replace the telegraph. Folk harvested a living from desert soil, blasted it from solid rock, or pedaled wares and services to those who did. Law and order—or its opposition—depended on a man's skill with a gun and his nerve facing one. As slow as progress was, Trace watched it outpace him from his stationary position of vigilance.

A refreshing aroma, bold yet sweet, floated on the breeze, contending with the pervasive scent of manure. The dog yipped and thumped its tail against the wooden walk. Trace followed its pointing nose and saw a lady strolling toward him, carrying a parasol. She was a mirage in pastels, soothing to thirsty eyes. He ordered the animal to stay put, then shook his head as the hound scooted toward her on its belly tortoise-style, squeaking like a wagon wheel. She bent to pet the mottled pelt, never minding that the dusty fur would soil her lace gloves. When her attention turned to the mutt's master, Trace felt a familiar, inevitable ache upon meeting her sky-blue gaze. She answered his frown with a sunny smile. "How do you do, Trace?"

"Fine, thank you, Holly." He wished she wouldn't check in on him. "How's Jerrod?" Her husband's name still left a bitter taste in Trace's mouth.

She told him they'd been to visit the farm—meaning the Malloy homestead—so he was obliged to ask after his brother and sister. Holly said that Tyler, Aimee, and Tyler's wife Beth were all in good health, then added, "Little Josiah is getting big." She didn't tell him he ought to go see for himself, that he was long overdue to visit his kin.

"Did Casey come back with you?"

She hummed an affirmation. "He seems quite smitten with Aimee." Trace nodded, ignoring the arching of her brow. "I know he's eager to have her hand, but she still misses her husband."

"They were married a day," said Trace.

"The heart doesn't let go so easily," she replied. He wondered if she was still talking about his sister. He was relieved when she let the subject drop but cared even less for that which she picked up. "Do you reckon you'll win the election?"

Trace shifted his shoulders. Previous Arizona Territory governor, Frederick Augustus Tritle, had appointed him to his office, but only his constituents' vote would let him keep it. Unfortunately, he had an opponent in the running for sheriff. Easton Stine had money with which to schmooze town officials, fancy speeches, and fashionable attire, but Trace understood the common folk, came from their lot. "I reckon voters will decide the best man for the job," he said.

Holly invited him to supper. When he made his excuses, she offered to bring him a leftover slice of pie. Trace hadn't the heart to tell her he didn't want it.

The dog whimpered to see her leave. "Go on," said Trace. "See her home." The hound rallied at his call to action, bounding to catch up. Trace watched them go, tail swinging and lilac dress and brunette curls swaying, then winced as the pin on his badge pierced his palm. He reaffixed it to his vest and sucked away the drop of blood, noting that he needed a shave. He was heading back inside when heralded by a man racing toward him from the opposite direction Holly had gone, his face as red as the hair curling beneath his Stetson.

"Sheriff. Hennessy's in town." Deputy Casey Horne imparted his news amid gasps for breath, finally getting out that he'd spied the outlaw hitching his horse in front of The Old Mare.

Trace tamed the thrum of excitement in his breast, endeavoring to set a calm example for his subordinate. "Unless he's headed into the bank with six desperadoes, you needn't have made such a ruckus. Remember, keep a level head."

"Don't get dead," the younger man finished.

"Tell me the count. Are they heeled?"

"Just the woman," reported Casey. "She has a Winchester."

Trace nodded then continued into the jailhouse. His deputy followed as readily as the hound. Trace opened the safe and passed him the gun-belt and badge he'd advised Casey to leave behind when he called on Aimee.

"You want me to go with you, sheriff?"

Trace winced at the giddy pitch to the young man's voice. "I can handle this one." To his credit, Casey didn't protest. Trace reckoned the deputy was as eager as Trace had been when he first pinned on the badge, consumed with righteousness at the sanctity of his office. *Del, you didn't tell me it would fade so fast.*

***

The Old Mare was revitalized under ownership of Easton Stine, a newcomer to the territory who bought prominence in Prospect by acquiring several mining claims and purchasing the town's iconic saloon-bordello. He kept those features which gave the establishment its character, including the mahogany bar, the nude painting above it, and the horseshoe-shaped balustrade lining the second-floor balcony. He replaced the missing batwing doors, brought in better booze, and added gaming tables with house dealers. The Mare's main attraction, its prostitutes, were also freshened with new talent and risqué uniforms. The place still served the same caliber of clientele but became more efficient at parting men from their hard-earned dollar.

Evelyn Deveraux followed her new boss into the bordello where she'd worked after being let go from a classier parlor house across town. Evelyn had undergone her own alteration, trading stockings and corset for trousers and a man's shirt. She now carried a rifle to discourage the advances of men she had to entertain as part of her previous occupation. But she still turned heads, her figure no less alluring under coarse coverings, her auburn mane drawing eyes from every corner of the room. She tugged down the brim of her hat to shadow her face, the resulting mystique only serving to distinguish full lips. Her transformation was not the one she set out to affect when she left home, yet she was close to gaining something beyond her expectations, an independence she could not have imagined at sixteen.

Wyatt Hennessy, self-possessed leader of the highwaymen who once rallied to notoriously savage Silas Kelly, claimed an empty table, motioning for Evelyn to take the seat to his left. She sat sideways, standing her lever-action on its butt and leaning the barrel against her chair's back. She wouldn't have to turn her head to keep the saloon doors in her line-of-sight.

Wyatt lifted his hat and ran a hand back and forth over cropped, dark hair. "Relax," he said, light brown eyes cutting toward her, "or you'll tip your hand." He'd given her the same advice when they'd met over poker under those very oil lamps. After nearly two years at The Old Mare, she'd turned to liquor for putting up with the men and to cards for an out. She bet all, staking her future, losing the game but winning his ear. Now he was giving her a last chance at a new life.

Evelyn rested her elbow on the tabletop and forced herself to comply, subduing nerves and suppressing the postural habits formed from years wearing a corset. A scantily dressed waitress sashayed up with two glasses, whisky, and a message that Stine would receive them shortly. Wyatt instructed her to leave the bottle. He slid one glass toward Evelyn and filled it to the brim, then raised his own in toast. "To making our own luck," he said.

They were on their second round when the woman returned to inform them her boss awaited their company in his upstairs office. "Tell him we'd be obliged if he would join us down here." The saloon girl blinked as if Wyatt had suddenly started speaking Apache. Her befuddled gaze moved to Evelyn who could only offer a sympathetic smile.

Wyatt was pouring their third round when Stine emerged from the last room at one end of the horseshoe balcony. Narrowed eyes of steel-gray scrutinized them as he adjusted the coat on his stout frame. He smoothed back dark, oiled hair going silver at the temples before following the curved oaken banister to the stairs.

Stine wore a black suit with gold cufflinks that clashed with the badge of town marshal on his coat. He didn't encumber himself with a gun, preferring to delegate the more physical responsibilities of his position to subordinates. He took the chair to Wyatt's right, across from Evelyn. Picking up her glass, he raised it, signaling the waitress that they needed another. She brought it directly and he sent her off with a pat on her ruffle-covered derriere.

"I could provide more comfortable accommodations upstairs," he said, topping off their glasses. "Surely, the lady would prefer some wine."

Evelyn tried to ignore him, her focus on each swing of the double doors. As she watched, Trace Malloy entered. The sheriff was unmistakable even through the haze of cigar smoke. He had a brawny build more befitting a pitchfork than the six-shooter on his hip. Evelyn would recognize that cleft chin anywhere, even with straw-colored bristle. His eyes sought them immediately, no doubt tipped off to her and Wyatt's arrival in Prospect. She signaled her boss with a touch on his arm as Malloy took a stool at the bar.

"We've got preparations to see to," Wyatt told Stine. "If the arrangements are made." Malloy stared at the group, making no effort to be inconspicuous. Evelyn shivered as the sun-flecked hazel orbs peering out from the shade of his hat seemed to glow with their own light. She took a gulp of liquid courage and fluttered her lashes at the blatantly glowering lawman. At their present distance, he wouldn't notice, but it made her feel bold.

"I've fulfilled my end," said Stine. "But I'd like to request the operation take place in Pinal County."

Wyatt shook his head. "The target will be slowest coming to the top of Badger Hill."

"The canyon bottleneck will work just as well," said Stine. "The stage mustn't cross the county line."

The disagreement drew Evelyn's attention to the men at the table. Stine's expression was expectant, awaiting acquiescence. Wyatt's jaw moved like he was chewing. "I reckon an adjustment can be made."

"Excellent." Stine grinned. Business concluded, he offered Wyatt a whore before leaving town. "Of course, none are as naturally beautiful as our present company." Evelyn stiffened as his gaze wandered over her. "If you tire of roughing it, I would be pleased to offer you a position back here. I was exceedingly sorry that you left The Mare before I acquired her." When she didn't answer, he turned back to Wyatt. "Does she wear bloomers or a union suit?"

Wyatt said, "I don't sleep with my men." Stine chuckled, but Evelyn sat up taller. She knew the distinction was contingent upon her passing initiation into the outlaw gang. She remembered to glance at Malloy. Her breath caught upon finding the stool empty. Her heart kicked up its rhythm when she spotted him making his way toward them.

The fluttering in her stomach was maddening and only intensified as he side-stepped customers, his golden eyes seemingly locked on her. Approaching in a manner less wary than resolute, he came to stand over the table.

"State your business here." His stance suggested he was ready to draw if need be.

"Just came to wet my whistle." Wyatt indicated the whisky. "Join us?"

The sheriff's scowl shifted from him to Evelyn. "Town Ordinance Number Nine prohibits carrying a firearm within Prospect limits."

"Town matters fall under my jurisdiction," interjected Stine, "not yours."

"If you won't arrest them, I will," countered Trace.

"It would behoove you to learn some diplomacy, Mr. Malloy," said Stine. "This brutish ideality might have a place in an unsophisticated shantytown, but Prospect has a prosperous future. Come next election, you might find the constituency opting for more refined representation."

"Folk respect action, not talk," the sheriff replied. "And if you aim to enforce the laws, you ought to educate yourself as to what they are."

Stine stood and adjusted his suit. "Mr. Hennessy is unarmed and therefore free to go." Wyatt stood and ignoring Malloy, they shook hands.

The bandit leader turned to the sheriff. "You sure you can handle her?" He smirked as he stepped around him on his way out.

Evelyn waited until Malloy's eyes were on her, then slid her hand up the barrel of the Winchester, away from the trigger. "I don't feel safe without it," she said, pouting.

"I'm bound by law to take you in. Confiscate her weapon, Marshal." Evelyn noted the biting emphasis he put on the title.

"Allow me." Stine took the rifle as if it were a chivalrous gesture, offering Evelyn his other hand to help her up. He bowed and brushed his lips over her fingers before releasing her hand. "My offer stands."

Malloy gestured toward the door and fell into step behind her. Many appreciative eyes followed her exit. Outside, Wyatt was readying his horse, tethering Evelyn's sorrel behind the bay.

"Stine's not wrong," he called. "If a man is good, the only law he need heed is that of his conscience."

"Says the criminal." Malloy indicated for Evelyn to proceed. She walked tall toward the jailhouse, the sheriff shadowing her.

2

Trace felt less like a lawman escorting his prisoner than a bull being led by the nose as Evelyn struck out ahead of him, boots clacking against the boardwalk planks. He couldn't help but notice how her feminine form filled out a pair of trousers, how they made her legs look longer than any skirt could. Her hair swung as she strutted, a wave of red commanding attention, the sway of her hips prompting a chorus of low whistles in their wake. Though accustomed to the afternoon heat, Trace's throat went dry and he felt himself begin to sweat. He had the untimely realization that he was long overdue for a night with a woman.

He locked her in the cell, oddly relieved to have the bars between them. Casey's mouth fell open as they entered and remained agape. Trace could hardly blame him, not with the way Evelyn sprawled on the cot like it was a divan, with one foot on the mattress and one on the floor. She tucked an arm behind her head which pulled the cotton shirt taut across her breasts. He couldn't fault the man, but he was annoyed all the same.

"Horne." Sheriff barked and deputy snapped to attention. "Head home for the day," said Trace. "See if your pa needs any help with his patients." Dentist Jacob Horne had moved his family to Prospect and set up a practice the previous winter. Since then, he had no shortage of work. He encouraged his son to study the profession, hoping he'd give up aspirations of becoming a lawman, but Casey still subscribed to a young man's dreams of glory. Though he could relate to his deputy, Trace secretly sided with the elder. When his sister was ready to remarry, he preferred she choose a dentist's apprentice over another gunslinger. Looking abashed, the young man didn't question the dismissal.

"Alone at last," said Evelyn. "Now that you have me here, what are you going to do with me?"

Trace doubted she was referring to the twenty-five dollar fine she'd face once he got her before Judge Foster. "You ever use that gun?"

She sat up, rolling off her spine, dropping her foot to the floor. "You ever use that one?" She gave him an impish smile.

He waited for her gaze to rise from his crotch to his face then said, "It's not the way for a woman to keep safe."

Green eyes flashed. "If I kept a derringer in my bosom, would that be ladylike enough for you?"

"This talk don't become you." He reckoned her defensiveness was due to having just been abandoned by Wyatt Hennessy. He'd first met Miss Deveraux after the shootout during which two of the three Kelly brothers were killed. His first act as sheriff had been to interview her as a witness. She'd admitted being all set to abscond with the deviant Silas Kelly. She hadn't seemed like the type. She still didn't now that she was mixed up with Silas's successor. Trace felt there was more to her, an underlying elegance, a veiled intelligence. He reckoned desperation had her tagging along with ruffians. "It might not seem like you have options," he said, "but you do."

Apparently, she had no comeback because she averted her eyes and fell silent. Watching her gather her thoughts, the lowered lashes and hint of vulnerability did more for Trace than suggestive poses and bawdy innuendo. He sensed it would be disastrous to let on that she'd finally affected him, so he collected his shaving kit from a desk drawer, hooked his hat on a peg on the wall, and went around back of the jailhouse where there was a water trough and pail.

He started to fill the bucket, dumped it, and dunked his whole face into the cool water. He remained stooped over, dripping back into the trough, the fever in his blood extinguished.

With a clear head, he opened the kit. He took his time, to avoid cutting himself, but mostly to think. He decided the best Miss Deveraux could do for herself was to find a husband. Men still outnumbered women in Prospect, as in most mining towns. Trace was certain plenty would be elated to secure such a wife, and most would have no qualms about her past. Problem was, she seemed to gravitate toward the dangerous ones.

Trace's sister had fallen for one such desperado. Josiah Wyland had lived and inevitably died by the gun, leaving her with child. Trace could never understand what drew a good woman to a bad man.

He was packing his kit when the spotted hound returned, coming around the building with its nose to the ground and tail wagging. Trace greeted it with a scratch behind the ears.

***

As soon as Malloy was gone, Evelyn dropped her head into her hands. Her sigh ended with an oath. He was wrong. She didn't have options. What she had was a chance, which she warned herself not to squander. Malloy was no fool, but she had to believe he was fallible, just as she had to believe Wyatt wouldn't give her a test she couldn't pass. Her past qualified her for this assignment. Her future depended on it.

Evelyn heard footsteps. She squared her shoulders, tossed back her hair, and prepared to try again. But the next figure to come through the door wasn't the stoic lawman. A pretty, young woman stared at Evelyn. "Where's Trace?" she said, then blushed and corrected herself. "Sheriff Malloy."

"Around back, making himself presentable." The lady scowled, not taking her meaning. "Shaving," Evelyn elaborated. Apparently, he knew he had company coming. "Come in. I won't bite." Evelyn knew most men would perceive her windswept hair and assume her wanton, but a woman of fashion and manners would see her only as wild.

She carried a parcel, something wrapped loosely in cloth, across the room and set it on the sheriff's desk. The scent of gardenia followed her. Evelyn watched her like the animal her cage implied. The woman's soft complexion and stylish curls marked her as conscientious of her beauty. Her clothing suggested a generous allowance, but she lacked the severity of high-class breeding. Evelyn saw nothing to indicate the lady would be above setting her cap at the good sheriff and decided watching her might offer some clue as to how to handle him.

***

Returning with the dog, Trace stopped short at the sight of the two women. "Mrs. Kelly," he said, careful to keep to the boundaries of propriety with his prisoner in earshot.

Holly said, "I brought you pie."

"Smells good." All he could smell was her perfume.

There was a moment of palpable silence in the jailhouse. Then Holly and Trace spoke at once. "I wanted to talk to you," she began. He said, "Now's not a good time."

Holly glanced at Evelyn and straightened her spine while the other woman leaned a shoulder against an iron bar. Trace thought how improbable it seemed that they came from similar backgrounds. Holly found work at The Wishing Well, a saloon and parlor house in Tucson, after coming west from Chicago. Deveraux had been a jewel in Prospect's own Treasure Room before moving to The Old Mare. Yet they were so different. Holly was sweet as a strawberry blossom. Evelyn had the thorns and dusky allure of a desert rose.

"Another time," Holly agreed, concern and disappointment clouding her cornflower eyes. She paused as she passed him in the doorway and raised her hand, almost touching his newly shaven cheek before thinking better of it. The dog whined and trailed after her without indication from either of them.

"There's history between you and her," said Evelyn.

"It's over." Trace sat in the chair behind his desk, pushing the parcel aside. He loaded a leaf of paper into the typewriter, making ready to compose his report on Miss Deveraux's arrest.

"How often does she bring you pie?" Evelyn shot him a suggestive smile.

Trace glowered at her over the blocky, black machine. "Holly is loyal to her husband." He began to hunt-and-peck the keys, careful where he stabbed his thick farmer's fingers.

"Bet he wasn't her first allegiance," said Evelyn. "You didn't thank her." His index finger slipped and punched two letters at once. He gave her a sharp look which she paid no mind. "Bet she would have accepted a kiss."

"I would never compromise her honor."

"Morality is a bore of a virtue."

"We can't all be as despicable as Silas Kelly." He poked more keys, awaiting her retort. When none came, he glanced up.

"I can't say much to defend him," she conceded with a shrug.

"What did you see in him?" Trace reclined in the chair, curiosity piqued.

"Possibility," said Evelyn. "He challenged me to imagine a different life."

"One in which you wouldn't have to barter your body?"

"That I might live on my own terms, beholden to no man."

"Except him," said Trace.

Evelyn shook her head. "He made me no promises, offered no protection, asked no exchange of favor. I think he was lonely." She ignored Trace's snort. "He wanted someone to share in his idea of freedom, someone who would revel in it as much as he."

It didn't coincide with Trace's recollection of Silas's character. Incredulously, he asked, "He told you that?"

"No," she said. "He told me he killed his father."

Trace didn't know how to respond. The death of the town marshal of Promise, Arizona had been attributed to attack by Apaches. Trace and the eldest Kelly brother had both turned sixteen that summer. If what Evelyn said was true, the murder was Silas's first kill.

Trace decided he needed a drink. He rifled through a desk drawer until he found a flask. He took a long pull of whisky and pondered the unexpected insight into his childhood nemesis.

"Any chance I could get a swig of that?"

Under normal circumstances, he would have denied her. But she'd just opened up to him after an afternoon void of cooperation. He didn't want her to resume the charade, so he brought her the flask. She stood to receive it, and he handed it through the cell bars, wondering what else she might divulge.

She raised the container to her lips and her eyes to his. He couldn't decide which was more attractive, her lips pursed over the flask's opening or her pale green eyes rimmed with heavy lashes. She tipped her head back, and his gaze fell to her throat as she swallowed. Without meaning to, he asked, "And Hennessy, what do you see in him?"

"Wouldn't you rather know what I see in you?" She smiled, a slow curving of lush lips. "I think you're attracted to the forbidden, to whatever tests your resolve." She stepped closer to the bars, closer to him, skimmed her fingers down one bar and back up. "You allow her to bring you pie, but you don't eat it," she said. "I reckon you like temptation."

Trace pointed to the whisky as if too parched to ask for it, and she passed it back. "You have a talent for seduction, Miss Deveraux," he said, capping the flask. "Perhaps you ought to forego the outlaw life and accept Stine's proposal."

She actually cringed at his words. Her lip curled and revulsion flooded her eyes. Before he could make sense of her reaction, she turned her back and stepped away.

Trace retreated to his desk but knew he didn't have the fortitude to focus on paperwork. He dragged his chair out front of the jail and watched dusk darken the town.

3

Evelyn paced the cell which seemed to grow smaller with each turn. Somehow, she had underestimated Malloy, and now her opportunity was fading with the sun.

Once again, she'd gambled everything, this time staking her future on her knowledge of men. But Malloy had proven different. He possessed a capacity for restraint she had little occasion to observe. In her previous profession, men came to her with control loosely held, perfectly ready to get their money's worth, needing little in the way of seduction. With the sheriff, Evelyn had aimed for provocation shy of solicitation, counting on him to meet her. She'd missed her mark.

She flopped onto the cot and closed her eyes, replaying every innuendo. He wasn't dense. He wasn't immune. She didn't believe him as commendable as he pretended—or strived—to be.

Her thoughts came around to the one impediment she hadn't anticipated. It was worse than indifference, she concluded, worse than resolve. Trace Malloy was in love with that Holly woman. Evelyn groaned in disgust. She owed her failure to rotten luck. She wondered if this time Wyatt would leave her to it.

***

Trace pondered what her restlessness indicated, what the look on her face had signified. She'd turned from him as if his suggestion were unspeakable, as if he'd addressed a virgin instead of a seasoned strumpet. Even if he misconstrued Stine's offer, she had no more case for offense than he.

She impugned his honor as a law officer while he was doing his damnedest to deter her from a life of crime and its inevitable end. Worse, she insulted Holly, whose rise she ought to aspire to.

He went back inside, intending to set her straight, only to find her asleep. He stood at the bars, watching the rise and fall of her chest as his own tightened with longing. He needed to make a trip to Phoenix soon or perhaps Tucson. It was a self-imposed rule that he never go to the cathouses in Prospect for his recreation, lest it manifest a conflict of interest. Besides, The Treasure Room was too rich for his pocketbook, and he'd rather ride forty miles than give a nickel to Easton Stine.

His prisoner moaned softly as if to punctuate his need. He extinguished the oil lamp and settled onto his cot. His eyes adjusted and he found moonbeams through the window were adequate to illuminate her features. Her dark hair seemed to absorb the light while her skin reflected it, shining ethereal in silver hue. Clouds passed over and night engulfed the room.

***

Evelyn awoke and sensing she wasn't alone, sat up. "What time is it?" she asked the darkness.

"Late."

She peered in the direction of the voice coming from the cot outside the cell. "Do you sleep here?"

"Sometimes."

She heard movement, a brush of clothing as he stood, a creak of the floorboards under his weight. She braced herself for the flare of a match, expecting him to light candle or lamp. It didn't come.

She too stood, groping for the bars, using them to orientate herself. She wondered if he could see. She listened for him but heard only her own heartbeat.

Then a gray glow filled the room, brightening to silver as clouds unveiled the moon. They stood diagonal, to one another's right, each facing the bars. She regarded him—beyond her power to influence—noting that the moon gave a marble quality to his chiseled jaw, making him seem statuesque. His hair, tawny in sunlight, appeared ashen.

The shadows surrounding them encroached and Evelyn blinked before realizing the clouds were gathering again. She closed her eyes and opened them to blinding darkness.

He shifted. She couldn't tell in which direction until his hand contacted hers. At first, she thought it unintentional, but as his touch lingered, her pulse quickened in anticipation. His fingers fondled, moving up and down the length of hers, drawing circles on her knuckles, tracing the bones in her hand. She expected him to break the connection, but his hand skimmed over her wrist, followed her arm to her shoulder, and slid beneath her hair, cupping the back of her neck.

His other hand found her waist then slipped around to the small of her back. He guided her forward until her pelvis met the cold iron barrier. He held her tight against it, against him.

His nose nudged her cheek before his mouth found hers. His lips moved and Evelyn felt the breath of words that didn't reach her ears. She started to ask what he'd said, but his tongue breached her lips, silencing her.

His hunger sparked hers. Appetites flared. Her hands clutched his shirt before eagerly moving to his belt. He growled when it turned loose. His fingers clenched the back of her skull as his tongue lashed hers. The hand on her back gripped lower as he strained to force them closer than the bars would permit. Evelyn felt a ball of warmth hit her belly as though she'd downed another shot of whisky. Before she could turn him loose, he released her and stumbled back out of reach.

Again, she froze, listening and waiting, trying to tame her ragged breath. She heard his rasp. There was a jangle as he fastened his belt. The door creaked and slammed. When the moon shone again, Evelyn was alone.

***

Trace stormed along the boardwalk, boots thundering over wooden planks, fists and jaw clenched. Folk scrambled out of his path. Any who hailed him were ignored. He exploded through the double doors at The Old Mare, paying no heed to the attention he drew, and marched up to the bar.

"Whisky," he barked at the bartender. The old man raised an eyebrow but poured without a word. Trace threw back the shot. "Another." He sucked it down, then planted his hands on the mahogany surface and waited for the lightning in his blood to dissipate. Finding the drink ineffectual, he scanned the crowd, looking for trouble. He was spoiling for a fight, hankering for a fuck. But the customers had all gone back to their recreation. His gaze roamed over the painted ladies whose costumes left little to the imagination, over gamblers engrossed in their game, over miners almost too weary to heft their mugs. He sat, but his eyes continued to wander, seeking a man as bad-tempered as he, mean enough to make a good fight.

"Buy me a drink, sheriff?" One of the prostitutes took the stool beside Trace, sitting with her back to the bar. She put her elbows on the counter and arched her spine, giving him a considerable view. He signaled the bartender which encouraged her to place a hand on his thigh. She massaged the muscle, working her way toward his groin. He spotted Stine on the horseshoe-shaped balcony, overlooking his business. Trace felt a prick of irritation when the town marshal smiled smugly and gave him a nod.

When the woman's touch skimmed his crotch, a vision of Evelyn flashed in his mind. He sucked in a breath and swatted her hand away. "I'm only good for a drink."

The opportunity Trace was waiting for came when a burly card player slammed a meaty fist down on a table across the room hard enough to splinter the wood and make the liquor glasses leap. The man rose from his chair to loom over the other players as a hush came over the crowd. Trace slid off his stool. He'd found his huckleberry. He moved through the saloon, eyes targeting the brute's ruddy face, cracking his knuckles in anticipation.

Before he could reach the table, he ran into a hand that met with the center of his chest. He looked down, following the arm to discover the man to whom it was attached. Jerrod Kelly regarded him with cool green eyes. "You made quite the entrance," he said.

There was a time when Trace would have turned his ire upon the youngest Kelly brother with relish, a time when Jerrod would have obliged him. That rivalry ended the day Holly took the name Kelly. Trace didn't want a one-sided fight any more than he wanted a bought woman, so when Jerrod's hand moved to his shoulder, he allowed himself to be redirected back to the bar.

The crowd resumed its usual volume, the gambling dispute amounting to nothing more than a show of frustration. Trace's anger faded with the sobering realization that he might have injured someone to ease his own.

Jerrod called the bartender over to pour them a round. "So, what's got your back up?"

Rather than admit to being driven horn-mad by his prisoner, Trace said, "Why aren't you home with your wife?"

Jerrod told him he was riding shotgun for the stage the next day, filling in for another man. They'd met at the local watering hole to discuss details for the run.

A few years ago, the Kelly brothers were the sort the stage lines needed protection against. In its heyday, their gang included some of the most cutthroat crack-shots in the territory, as violent as they were proficient. But as Rook Kelly's controlling nature clashed with Silas's chaotic one and he began seeking power on both sides of the law, a rift formed between the brothers. It culminated in a bloody showdown that robbed Trace of his retribution.

Jerrod had his own reasons for parting ways with his brothers. He'd mostly put that life behind him since marrying Holly, except for the occasional lawful gun-for-hire gig. He remained one of the most respected gunfighters in Arizona.

Trace declined another drink, deciding his best course was to get some sleep and let the other man be on his way. Jerrod paid and they bid one another, "So long."

The boarding house common rooms were empty past mealtime. Trace climbed creaky stairs and shuffled down a narrow hall to his room. He didn't bother with a candle. He locked the door and hung his gun-belt on the knob. He groped for the single bed, a heavy feather mattress on a rickety frame, then tugged off his boots, stripped down to his underwear, and lay back.

Still angry with himself for crossing a line reaching through those bars, he wasn't drowsy enough to fall directly asleep. The dark reminded him of the kiss, and his cock swelled at the memory of her taste. Knowing that the sooner he took care of his need, the sooner he could sleep, he pulled a handkerchief from beneath his pillow.

He stared into the pitch black and allowed an image of Evelyn to take shape in his mind's eye. He envisioned her naked, spread out on a bed of night clouds, skin luminescent as the moon, hair splayed all around. Topaz eyes peered at him through thick lashes. She opened her thighs, inviting his gaze to follow shimmering limbs to a shadowy apex. "Wider," he rasped, indulging in the fantasy. With a wicked turn of her lips, she complied. He remembered her moan, imagined his name in the same throaty tone.

Trace vowed his indiscretions were limited to that evening, that dawn would find his creed intact. Then he reached into the folds of his union suit and took himself in a firm hold.

***

Trace awoke the next morning, unease already forming in the back of his mind. He opened his eyes and bolted upright. His gun-belt hung from the doorknob. His clothes littered the floor. He rummaged through them, knowing he wouldn't find what he sought. His keys to the jail were missing.

He rushed to dress, grabbing up the wrinkled garments rather than root through dresser drawers. He jammed his feet into boots, cussing under his breath, berating himself for his carelessness. Last night, the memory of Evelyn's urgent hands had been a guilty pleasure. In the cold light of day, he felt only humiliation and self-contempt. He snatched his gun-belt off the knob, slammed the door behind him, and pounded down the stairs. He blew through the common room where other boarders were assembling for breakfast, and hit the street running.

He knew in his gut what he'd find upon reaching the jailhouse, though he hoped he was lucky enough to be wrong. As deserved, he discovered the cell door ajar, his keys dangling from the lock. Adding insult to injury, she'd stolen his hat off the peg on the wall. He noticed because hers had been left in its place.

4

The sun rose behind Evelyn, projecting her shadow and that of her horse ahead. Wyatt had hitched the sorrel near the edge of town for her to find on her way out of Prospect. Still a novice horsewoman, she'd been forced to ride cautiously through the night, following the base of the hills in a northwestward arc toward the Gila River, watching for landmarks she could recognize by the glow of a fickle moon. Her neck ached from the countless times she'd peered over her shoulder expecting to glimpse a posse on her tail.

When blocky structures materialized on the horizon, she dug in her heels and sent her mount galloping toward an imaginary finish line. The rah of wind between buildings, the clap of loose shutters, and the skipping of tumbleweeds down an empty street was all the fanfare that greeted her. The dusty main drag and ruins that lined it were all that remained of auspicious Promise. After a flood washed away most homes and businesses, survivors founded the new town of Prospect.

Evelyn ventured into the abandoned settlement, her horse's hoofbeats the only sign of life. The desert had exacted its toll. Wood planks warped, making gaps in walls and ripples in roofs. Grime fogged the windows that were still intact, but many had fallen from deformed frames. Either pot shots defaced two buildings on opposite sides of the street, or a gun war had been waged from them. Evelyn shuddered to think of the latter.

She started to worry that she was alone with whatever ghosts inhabited the town's remains, that she had come too late and Wyatt hadn't waited, or that he'd discounted her and never shown. Then she spotted a lean figure watching her approach from the shade. He stepped forth as she vaulted from the saddle.

"You made it," he said. "Just in time." He checked his pocket watch. "The stage leaves Prospect in forty-five minutes." His wry grin was split by a guffaw when she flung her arms around him. He shook his head while adjusting the stolen hat on hers. "Malloy must be madder than an old wet hen," he said. "And his day's about to get worse."

His horse was ready and waiting in an alley between buildings. He transferred her Winchester to the saddle sheath on her sorrel. Then they rode south, converging with the stage road.

Evelyn kept her horse at the bay's flank to avoid eating Wyatt's dust. The trail, two ruts carved by hooves and wagon wheels, snaked across the sage-dotted and cactus-treed expanse, disappearing into a small canyon. The maw narrowed into a winding red-rock chute hardly wide enough for three riders to travel abreast.

Around a particularly tight bend, the canyon opened for a spell before the next corner. Six men sat atop a crescent-shaped outcropping on the outer curve, hawking tobacco juice to pass the time. Wyatt and Evelyn added their mounts to the herd stashed in the dry gully behind the rocky hill and scaled the jagged mound to join their confederates.

Evelyn situated herself between Wyatt and Benjamin Bradford, the youngest of four scruffy, scrawny brothers in the outfit. He paused his trick-draw practice to offer her a lump of snuff and a brown-speckled grin. Evelyn suppressed a shudder. It seemed every other man who'd come into her bed at The Mare had a wad in his lip. Worse than their rank breath was the spittle that dribbled from slack jaws as each found his release.

"Listen up," said Wyatt. Checking his watch, he explained that the stage would have to slow down to navigate the canyon but would still be traveling as fast as the terrain allowed. There'd be at least one armed guard. "Deveraux will take the shot." Hearing this, some of the men grumbled. Wyatt caught her look of alarm. "Relax," he said. "You need only shoot the lead horse."

Though Evelyn practiced and Wyatt had described how to swing-through, she'd yet to shoot a moving target. The commotion of the approaching stage left no time to argue. Men worked bandanas up over their noses, making ready. Most were instructed by Wyatt to wait down by the horses. Evelyn lay on her belly on the rocks, propping herself up on her elbows, positioning the Winchester. Soon, she could feel a hum through the earth as the din of stampeding horses intensified. Wyatt was putting his trust in her. She'd passed her initiation but had yet to prove herself to the other men. This was her chance.

The train of horses rounded the canyon bend, drawing the wagon, backdropped by a storm of red dust. The racket echoed off the rock walls like thunder. Evelyn sighted, knowing she had only a small window of time in which to take the shot. If the horses rounded the next curve, the gang would be forced to pursue. She targeted the animal closest to her, staring down the barrel, picking a point at the base of its neck above churning legs. She wasn't sure whether her nerves made her quake or if it was only the vibrations up through the ground. To either side, small stones rattled loose and rained down both sides of the hill.

The moment came to fire. She touched her finger to the trigger, felt its resistance and hesitated, unprepared for the resistance in her heart. She had never killed a living creature, hadn't expected to have to shoot one so magnificent and noble. The horse appeared the same shade of chestnut as her own mount.

"Take the shot, Deveraux," warned Wyatt, putting his mouth near her ear. Another man seconded the command.

Her target was moving past when she fired. She closed her eyes and squeezed the trigger. The rifle kicked back into her shoulder. She didn't see the bullet ricochet off rock, but the explosion was followed by the cursing of men telling her she'd missed. For a split second, she was relieved despite her failure.

The shot gave away the ambush. Ben turned and skidded down the incline, hollering for the others to mount up. The stage driver bellowed at his team already rounding the next bend. Through billowing dust, Evelyn spied movement atop the carriage. Spinning in his seat, the guard leveraged his weapon to retaliate. Wyatt seized Evelyn's arm and hauled back as a shotgun blast disintegrated the rocky crest. They tumbled down the hillside together.

Bandits swung up into saddles and spurred horses. By the time Evelyn reached her mare, Wyatt was already mounted, pulling his six-gun and rushing to join the pursuit. She fumbled to get her rifle into its scabbard and clambered up into her own saddle. She clutched the reins as the sorrel charged into the fray.

Wheels and hooves churned up dirt into clouds gritty in Evelyn's eyes, chalky in her mouth, thickly clogging her nose. Gunshots filled the crevasse ahead. Men swatted equine rumps, gaining on their prey. It tested Evelyn's skill just to keep up. The wagon swayed toward one rock wall then back toward the other, while riders hung to either side, watching for an opportunity to advance.

A wiry bandit leapt from his horse to the back of the wagon. The guard aimed from his seat beside the driver. The bandit ducked, but the shot blasted off fingers and he plummeted into the wake of dust. Evelyn jerked her reins to avoid trampling him. The shotgun continued firing away at the pursuers, attempting to force them to keep their distance. A horse collapsed in a spray of dirt, its rider cartwheeling into the air.

When the stage swung to the right, coming within inches of the canyon wall, Wyatt coaxed his mount into the space on the left. The horse squealed and Evelyn screamed as the gap closed. The bay fell back just in time to avoid being crushed then bolted forward when the opening came again.

Evelyn saw Wyatt level his gun at the driver. She didn't hear the shot, but the man lurched from his seat and the wagon rocked as the body fell beneath the wheels. The tipping unseated the guard who dropped the shotgun to cling with both hands to the stage's frame. No longer under control, the team took a turn too sharp, too fast for the carriage. A wheel and corner impacted solid rock. The whole stage was swallowed in a wave of dirt and splintering wood. Evelyn didn't see what became of the guard. Her mount skidded to a halt and circled amid the confusion of shouting men and whinnying horses.

***

His prisoner was long gone. Trace reaffixed the ring of keys to his belt and gave the cell door a swift kick closed. He plucked Deveraux's hat off the peg, humiliation surging through him, then turned on his heel and marched straight to The Old Mare.

The bordello was deserted, its customers gone back to their labors, their pocketbooks depleted, its prostitutes gone home to rest, depleted in a different sense.

The old bar dog wiping glasses looked up as Trace strode in. "On the prod again," he mumbled. "Best pull your horns afore you get them stuck." Trace ignored him.

Upstairs, he stepped over a pile of musky bedding destined for the laundry. A maid was busy cleaning the rooms where the whores entertained. Trace entered Easton Stine's office without knocking. Freshly dressed and no doubt already tallying the night's profits, the businessman waved him in as if anticipating the interruption.

Trace said, "I'm here to collect Miss Deveraux's rifle."

"I don't have it." Trace half-expected to hear him say she'd retrieved it herself. Instead, Stine explained, "As Mr. Hennessy was leaving town, I saw no reason why he couldn't take possession of it."

"That weapon was evidence," said Trace.

"Come now," said Stine. "Do you truly intend to charge her?"

"I don't like you interfering in my business," said Trace.

Stine sneered. "I don't like you interfering in mine."

"I take the laws of this town and the safety of its citizens seriously. You disregard both by consorting with criminals."

"This town appointed me marshal," said Stine.

Trace shook his head. "You bought that badge. I want to know what business you had with Hennessy yesterday."

Stine said, "I could just as easily ask what you discussed over drinks with Jerrod Kelly last night." Before Trace could protest the comparison, he continued, "Speaking of criminals, your brother-in-law, I've heard tell, was as bad as they come."

Trace bristled at Stine's implication of hypocrisy. Before he could articulate a response, Stine signaled to someone over his shoulder. A nervous Deputy Horne appeared at Trace's elbow. "Telegram, sheriff."

"Let's hope it's a matter more deserving of your diligence," Stine said as Trace accepted the slip of paper.

Downstairs, Trace read the message. It wasn't addressed to him but to the Southern Pacific stage line. According to the telegram, the Prospect mud wagon destined for Tucson was an hour late to the half-way station, meaning it had met with trouble in the first twenty miles.

Trace wanted to think it was a simple breakdown, a broken wheel or lame animal, but the uneasy feeling in his gut wouldn't let him. Obviously, the line operator suspected foul play as well, having brought the news to the sheriff's office.

Trace instructed his deputy to procure a wagon and team from the livery and load up materials and tools for repairs. "Bring Doc Finch along, just in case." Casey dashed to comply. Trace started to follow but turned back toward the boarding house instead, heading for the boarders' stable to ready his own mount. His stride lengthened until he moved at a run. He'd remembered that Jerrod Kelly rode out of Prospect with the stage that morning.

***

Dust hung in the air, fine as smoke. Evelyn stood beside her horse, watching dazedly as men rummaged through the wreckage looking for the strongbox. A Bradford brother rode back in search of wounded. Another helped Wyatt free the stage's team from their harness. She reckoned she appeared not unlike the sorrel—body damp with sweat, mane dulled by dust, mud running from her nostrils.

Something moved at her feet. She blinked to discover a body blanketed by dirt. He'd been unconscious, still as the ground. Now he stirred only slightly, obviously injured. Dust powdered his skin, hair, and clothing. She opened her mouth to call for aid but closed it again when he opened his eyes. They were a familiar shade of green belonging to no one in the gang. She realized he must be the stage's guard. The holster on his hip was empty, the shotgun lost as well.

A cheer erupted when a man located the treasure box, and the others converged to help extract the booty. The wounded man lost consciousness again. Evelyn looked up to see Wyatt striding toward her. He came to stand opposite her, over the body.

"Recognize him?" He kept his voice low.

"He looks familiar." She was certain she'd seen him before.

"That's Jerrod Kelly." She looked again. Dust made his hair look brown rather than black, and it wasn't straight like his brother's but curled around his face and collar. She recalled his eyes were nearly the same shade of jewel green, more opaque than polished. Jerrod was attractive, but Silas had been beautiful.

A crack echoed off the canyon rock as the bandits took an ax to the ponderosa pine box. They worked bullion out around the iron strapping and loaded it into saddlebags. Wyatt gave the order to mount up. Evelyn shot him a surprised look.

"Let him be," he told her.

They took the stage road out of the canyon, leading the six extra horses along. After a few miles in the open, they split up. The wounded would go with one man to Maricopa. Twenty miles west of Prospect, it was the closest settlement with a doctor. Three others would take the stage team south toward Tucson then release them into the wilderness. Evelyn was to ride north with Wyatt. They'd all return to Promise via alternate routes.

"Why did you let him live?" she asked once they were alone.

"Don't know that he will." Wyatt shrugged. "Jerrod Kelly had a code. If the fight was fair, he wouldn't hesitate to kill. But he wouldn't shoot a man who was down."

Evelyn nodded. She wondered if Silas had such a rule, remembering Trace Malloy's condemnation. As if to confirm her doubt, Wyatt said, "His brothers weren't so discriminate."

5

The dust had settled by the time Trace guided his buckskin gelding into the mouth of the ravine. Wind howled against the stone cliffs above his head, but otherwise, there was silence throughout the canyon. Nevertheless, Trace pulled his revolver.

Casey had wanted to go with him, when he learned that Trace planned to ride ahead alone. "The doctor can handle the wagon. You might need backup." Trace told him he needed to scout ahead to collect evidence, that any highwaymen would be long gone. Truth was, he wanted to be able to prepare the young man. He knew Casey admired Jerrod Kelly as a marksman and had befriended him on recent visits to the Malloy farm.

Heavy carriages pulled by many-hooved teams had ground dirt into powder that blanketed the canyon floor. Vegetation was sparse. Around one corner, the trail skirted a rocky knoll that Trace reckoned made the perfect vantage point by which to launch an ambush. He dismounted and scaled the slope, discovering horse manure in the trough on the other side. He scanned the jagged terrain and spiny brush for evidence of gunfire. A glint drew his eye to a single casing. It was the size used in a Winchester. He pocketed the brass and remounted.

Around a craggy bend, he discovered a downed horse. The shot imbedded in its hide suggested return fire from the stage. Trace felt a glimmer of hope. Perhaps the defense had discouraged the attackers. The mud wagon might have made it to the station after all. But then he came across the corpse of the stage driver, identified by the leather gauntlets he used to grip the reins. Around another corner was the wreckage of the coach itself.

The wagon was on its side, one wheel smashed from collision with a rock outcropping, the frame fractured upon impact. A glance inside confirmed the strongbox had been hacked open and looted. Trace peered under and around the wreckage, dreading the discovery of a certain body, alarmed at its absence. He clambered atop the stage and surveyed the surrounding ground, searching for a blood trail or any definitive clue among the hoof and footprints, bewildered until he spotted a human form fifteen paces back, lying near the canyon wall.

Trace hopped down and approached the still body. The eerie silence of the scene augmented the dread twisting his gut. He imagined facing Holly, telling her that her husband was dead.

He crouched at Jerrod's side. The man lay chest down, one arm beneath him, one along his side, a knee cocked as if he'd tried to crawl. Breath stirred the dirt. Trace fetched his canteen, wet a handkerchief, and mopped the side of his face. Jerrod came to with a prolonged moan. Green eyes cracked open.

"Dare I move you?" Trace took Jerrod's grunt for an affirmative. He rolled him onto his side while the injured man hissed through gritted teeth, then onto his back. He wasn't shot or bleeding as far as Trace could tell. "Are your arms broke?" Jerrod raised his right in answer.

He spit curses, an encouraging sign, while Trace worked to get him propped up in the shade, against the canyon wall. By the time he was situated, the gunfighter was pale, winded, and clammy with sweat.

Trace positioned his canteen at the man's right side. "Haven't you got anything stronger?" wheezed Jerrod. Trace was tempted to press him for details regarding the robbery but decided he ought to wait until after Jerrod received medical attention. He left him for minutes at a time to search the area. He came across Jerrod's revolver, knocked from his hip holster, and the shotgun, its load spent. A mass of hoofprints led further into the canyon.

When echoes through the ravine alerted him to the wagon's arrival, Trace jogged back to meet it. He let the other men know what to expect, that the driver had been trampled and Jerrod injured. Casey wanted to know how many bandits the crack-shot had gunned down first. Trace said that he hadn't asked, that the gang had retrieved their wounded.

Together, they struggled to load the dead weight of the driver. At the crash site, they turned the wagon around, then Trace helped doctor and deputy lift the injured man as gently as they could manage. Jerrod endured it though pain stole his color and breath. Doc Finch kept a stoic face, but Casey winced in sympathy. Trace hoped his expression didn't betray his own discomfort. The wagon rattled away along the return route to Prospect, Casey driving while Finch attempted to keep his patient comfortable and the deputy quiet.

Trace followed the robbers' trail in the opposite direction to where it departed the stage road, diverging in three directions. He pursued the heavier tracks only to realize the highwaymen must have led the team into the desert only to free them as a diversion. By then, it was late afternoon. Begrudgingly, Trace turned back.

***

Upon returning to Prospect, Trace went directly to the Kelly home. He found Casey pacing the porch, awaiting his arrival. "The doc's still with him," the deputy reported as Trace dismounted.

"Did you return the wagon and mules? Bring the body to the coroner?" Casey nodded. "I'd be obliged if you'd see to my horse."

"Sure, sheriff." Trace handed over the reins and patted the younger man on the shoulder. "Meet me at the jail in the morning."

Trace inhaled and let out a deep breath, then quietly entered the house. It was small but comfortable for a couple who had yet to start a family and had more than pleased Holly. The front room was spacious enough for kitchen and parlor area. Trace followed the low light and sound of sniffling to a bedroom at the back.

Jerrod Kelly lay on the bed, paler now that he was sponged clean and stripped of clothing. A sheet covered him from the waist down. His exposed torso already showed bruising. The doctor had wrapped his ribs and set his left arm.

Holly sat on the edge of a chair, curls vibrating with her shaking shoulders. Hearing footsteps, she lifted her tear-streaked face and launched herself into Trace's arms with a sob. She clutched his shirt and burrowed her face into it, choking on the surge of emotion. Trace embraced her tentatively, far from immune to her need but aware that comfort would invite her to fall apart in his arms.

Finch packed up his medicine bag. "I'm leaving a bottle of laudanum," he declared. "He'll likely need it to sleep." He gave Holly a pitying glance. "She may take a few drops as well." Trace thanked him. He nodded and saw himself out.

Trace took ahold of Holly's shoulders and held her upright, striving to impart strength and calm at the risk of seeming unsympathetic. He drew her toward the door with the suggestion she make herself some tea. He turned back to find Jerrod's eyes open, watching him in a way that made Trace feel guilty.

"I know she brings you pie."

"I don't eat it," said Trace. The last thing he needed was Jerrod getting agitated over an old rivalry, thinking he'd try to steal Holly while the gunslinger was unfit to fight for her.

Jerrod coughed out a laugh then grimaced and clutched his ribs. "I'd rather you say that you and I are friends."

Instead, Trace said, "Tell me about the holdup."

"Messy," said Jerrod. He closed his eyes. Trace wasn't sure if he was recollecting or had fallen unconscious. "Not like Hennessy."

"It wasn't Hennessy?"

"It was, but he would have chosen Badger Hill over the canyon. Someone else is calling the shots."

"Did you recognize any of his crew?"

"The woman," said Jerrod. "Deveraux." He gave Trace a peculiar look. "I could swear she was wearing your hat."

Trace felt his neck redden. Just then, Holly returned with teacups on a tray. She hastened to give Jerrod a sip. When a tear escaped down her cheek, he brushed it away. She kissed him, a tender and desperate clinging of lips that Trace remembered well. For an instant, he thought he should be the one making accusations, except he'd forfeited that right. Jerrod had been there for Holly when Trace had not.

Trace declined a cup, saying that he must be going. Jerrod raised his hand, stopping him. "We were booked for passengers, but not one showed," he said, his voice weak. "The mail neither."

Trace nodded and turned to leave. Holly insisted on seeing him out. "There will be justice," he promised her as they moved down the short hall.

At the door, she took his hand in hers. "Be careful," she pleaded. There was something in her eyes that no longer belonged to him.

"Look after your husband," he said.

***

Trace studied the map on the jailhouse wall as Jerrod's words echoed in his mind. *Someone else is calling the shots*. "Who?" he asked aloud. The spotted hound raised its head from between its front paws and stared at him as if waiting for Trace to answer his own question.

He'd left the Kelly home and come there to sleep—the jail being closer than the boarding house—only to toss and turn to the extent the narrow cot would allow. His promise to Holly pressed on him. The empty cell taunted him.

We were booked for passengers but not one showed. The mail neither. Trace turned from the wall to pace. "Any ideas?" The dog's eyes followed its master from one side of the room to the other. "The holdup didn't disrupt the mail." Trace halted.

"Meaning a U.S. Marshal won't be assigned to the case," he exclaimed. The dog didn't seem impressed. Trace continued to pace and muse. "No passengers means there'll be little cause for public outrage." Without it, Trace knew the town marshal wouldn't be bothered to act. "That leaves me." He returned to the map, found the canyon where the ambush had occurred, found Badger Hill. The trail of dashes that signified the stage route skipped over a solid line. "They wanted to stay in my jurisdiction," said Trace. The dog whined.

The revelation brought him back to his original question. Who was Hennessy partnered with, who had the resources to influence such variables as the passengers and mail? Trace could think of one man—Easton Stine. His next question was why? For the bounty? Robbery seemed an inefficient method for such a man to augment his wealth, especially since he'd have to split the loot with cutthroats. What else might he stand to gain? He recalled their exchange that morning, what he had said, what Stine had said. *I don't like you interfering in my business. I don't like you interfering in mine*. Absent-mindedly, Trace's hand moved to his vest, covering his badge. Was the businessman orchestrating mayhem to damage his opponent's reputation before the election? Did Easton Stine covet his office that much?

Trace's predecessor Rook Kelly had pretended to break ties with his older brother, had used his power as sheriff to his own advantage, had even used the position of public trust to secure Trace's sister as his bride (until she fled the marriage). If Easton Stine became both town marshal and sheriff, if he hired outlaws to enforce his authority as Rook had done, there'd be no one left in Prospect to oppose him. He had to know Trace wouldn't stand for such corruption. What was his plan? And was Evelyn Deveraux party to it?

Trace would have to wait for morning to seek answers. He returned to his cot and extinguished the light. And found it made no difference whether he closed his eyes or left them open. Two women waited for him in the darkness. That Evelyn might be Hennessy's lover, that the casing he found in the canyon might have come from her gun, made her no less desirable to him. And he had to assume both. So, he quelled his lust by recalling Holly's tears for her husband, her fear for his safety. But that only made him lonely for what he might have had, for what he'd given up. So, he thought of Evelyn again. One pushed the other from his mind, round and round, until he fell asleep.

6

A celebratory bonfire lit up the center of Promise, shooting sparks like fireworks and projecting ghoulish silhouettes against the false fronts. Drunken men fed the inferno dilapidated shutters and doors ripped from abandoned buildings, while in the old mercantile, bullion was divided into neat and equal piles on the counter. Evelyn watched the revelry from the boardwalk where the heat was less intense, where the shadows hid her dejection.

Two men stepped away from the blaze and stood side-by-side, their stance suggesting that they were draining their bladders. She couldn't see their faces, but the voices belonged to Ben and Beau Bradford. By their comments, she guessed they were referencing her. One said, "Those lips make a feller want to tip the velvet." His brother answered, "I'd like to tip something." He waggled his hips and they both laughed.

Wyatt's whistle summoned them to collect their shares. As they filed in, one man grumbled his opinion that Evelyn's miss ought to cost her take. She reckoned by the looks cast in her direction, most of amusement, the miss had lost her more than that. Lucas, who'd been chasing whatever painkillers he'd been administered in Maricopa with tequila, however many fingers he had left on his right hand wrapped in bandages, eyed her more severely. He slurred, "How you going to lay down a man if you can't kill a horse?" This prompted agreement from some and snickers from others. Someone muttered that she should skip the gunplay and offer a more pleasurable contribution. "I say it's the least she can do," said Lucas.

Evelyn retorted, "I have no problem shooting a man, and you can test me if you don't believe it."

"That's enough," said Wyatt. "A word, Deveraux." He walked out without waiting to see if she followed. Evelyn turned her back against whispers of crude speculation and trailed him across the street to the old jailhouse. The sturdiest building left in Promise and the only one with sleeping surfaces above the floor, Wyatt had claimed it as his quarters with Evelyn his bunkmate.

"You give them the wrong impression," she said, dropping to the slab of wood that served as her bed.

"You're safer for it," he replied, sitting opposite.

"I don't need chivalry," she said. "Silas Kelly would have let me protect myself."

"He would have run you raw, made his mark, and passed you around," said Wyatt, his voice turning sharp. "Don't believe me? Ask Lucas." Softer, he said, "I won't apologize for it." He pointed his chin at the sack in her hands. "How does it feel?"

"Undeserved," she admitted, setting aside her spoils.

"They're right. You're not cut out to be a road agent, Evelyn." She opened her mouth to protest, to promise him she'd redeem herself. "I need experienced men for what's coming," he said. "You've got a different set of skills."

She shot to her feet, felt the sting of tears as fear swallowed her anger. "I know I messed up." Pride kept her from falling to her knees and begging for a second chance.

"Today wasn't your fault." Wyatt took her hand, drew her to sit beside him on the other bench. "We never should have ambushed the stage in that canyon," he said. "It's on me for allowing Stine to alter the plan to satisfy his beef with the sheriff. All right?" Brown eyes intent, he waited for her to nod before releasing her hand.

"Why didn't you tell them that?"

"It would give the wrong impression."

He continued to look at her. She only had to shift her weight onto her hip and lean forward to align her lips with his. Almost touching, she lowered her eyes and waited.

"Evelyn," he said. "We're not all the same." She sat back, a little relieved, a little disappointed, more than a little skeptical. He asked, "How did you escape Malloy?"

"Hooked the keys." She blushed in spite of herself. "Off his belt."

Wyatt's lips twitched. "None of them could have done that." She laughed. "I've a mind to give you a special assignment," he said when she moved back across from him.

"What assignment?"

"I want you to deal with Malloy," he said. "Keep him out of our business, away from the town marshal."

"He's not going to fall for that again," said Evelyn.

"Then change your angle." Wyatt reclined on the bench, crossing his ankles, tucking an arm behind his head, and dropping his hat over his face. "I leave the means to you."

***

Trace got breakfast at the boarding house and picked up some spare clothes from his room, fetched and readied his horse, and loaded his saddlebags with goods from the general store, all the while considering how he might gain Evelyn Deveraux's cooperation. Next to Hennessy, she was the person most likely to know the extent of Stine's association with the gang. She'd been at the same table as them.

He reckoned the greater challenge would be tracking her down. Once he found her, he'd implement one of two strategies. He could threaten her with the consequences of her role in the ambush, forcing her to inform on her confederates to avoid the gallows. Or he could offer to help her, try to salvage the rapport begun in conversation through jailhouse bars before lust got the better of him. By one method or the other, he'd lead her to reason.

He was rooting around in the safe for extra ammo when Casey arrived. "Are we going after them then?" the deputy asked. "Should I round up a posse?"

Trace shook his head. "I need you here." Casey's shoulders slumped. "I know how you feel," Trace began.

"Aimee means to give me the mitten," the other man complained.

Trace scowled. "Did she say something?"

"No. But." Casey hung his head. "She married a man of action. A real gunfighter."

"And his death taught her a harsh truth about her choice. Aimee is a mother now. She needs a husband who can provide for his family, a good man to raise her son," said Trace. "Let her come to that realization. Be there when she does."

"Yessir," said Casey. Trace knew how the younger man felt, anxious to make a difference, to fulfill his life's purpose. He also knew the reality that awaited him.

"Del Cooper told me a lawman needs a self-sufficient wife able to carry on in his absence. Aimee is wiser for her past mistakes, more resilient for her loss."

"Why ain't you married, sheriff?"

Trace hadn't the inclination to explain his regrets. He said, "I really do need you here." He reckoned the outlaws had fled to a neighboring county to spend or stash their spoils, gone to one of the bigger towns where whores and other means of recreation were plentiful. But they might have a hideout in the surrounding wilderness, could know homesteaders who would harbor them. "If Hennessy or any of his outfit show in town, I want you to send word. I'll check telegraph offices wherever I pass through."

Casey nodded. "Which direction are you heading, sheriff?"

"South." Trace decided that The Wishing Well in Tucson was his best bet. Louanne Fitzgerald would tell him all she knew. Holly was like a daughter to the madame. "Do you know who all you're on the lookout for?"

"The Bradford brothers, Lucas, and Jim Jones." New to the territory, the four surviving brothers were wanted in Texas for rustling cattle. Also among the ranks were veterans of the old gang who'd stuck with Wyatt.

Trace nodded. "In particular, I want to know of any contact they have with Easton Stine."

"What's he got to do with it?"

"I don't know yet."

His deputy wished him luck. Trace mounted up and steered his horse along Main Street, meandering around slower traffic. There was one horse hitched outside The Old Mare. Trace's jaw dropped when he spied the white star just visible beneath the sorrel's forelock. "She's got grit," he mumbled, shaking his head. He turned his buckskin into the nearest alley and dismounted. It seemed he didn't have to go as far as Tucson after all.

***

Evelyn had been nude in a man's presence on numerous occasions, but she'd never felt as naked as she did in Easton Stine's domain without her gun. One of his employees relieved her of it upon arrival at the bordello. She didn't know the capacity in which the brute served Stine, if he was bodyguard, saloon enforcer, or one of the town marshal's police. Stine did business both public and personal out of the establishment. Since he also lived there, Evelyn was surprised to be kept waiting in his upstairs office.

The space at one end of the horseshoe-shaped second level had been remodeled to join two rooms via a set of French doors. Another set of doors opened the office to a balconet. Evelyn loitered in the latter doorway, watching the bustle down Main Street, her attention jumping from person to person, scanning for a brawny build and set jaw. She realized she was on the lookout for Trace Malloy. Getting the better of the sheriff had been the highlight of her days of late. She reckoned he would love an opportunity to make her pay for it. It was now her mission to give him the chance. The thought brought a smile to her lips.

"I'd give a silver dollar to know what you're thinking at this very moment." The noise below covered Stine's arrival, so she startled at his voice. He moved through the room with eyes trained on her, stopping to open the other set of doors, revealing the four-poster beyond. "Makes it seem bigger, doesn't it?" He rounded the desk, coming to stand within arm's length of her.

"Hennessy sent what was owed you." She gestured to the pouch on his desk.

"I'd hoped you were here because you reconsidered my offer," he said. "Your mouth looks delectable." His own wormed into a curve that made her skin crawl.

"Afraid not." Evelyn crossed her arms over her chest.

"Perhaps I can sweeten the deal." He raised a finger when she shook her head. "Hear me out," he said. "A lady ought to consider all her options." He spread his arms to encompass the suite, as if it would argue for him. Maybe it did, but Evelyn was familiar with the illusion.

Easton Stine's quarters were furnished with the same show of finery as The Treasure Room, a façade of sophistication glossing over crude reality. The truth was that Stine and the madame grew rich off the same money-for-pleasure transactions that took place in filthy back alleys for pennies. At the parlor house across town, the elite paid for a fantasy only to strip it down to the same carnal denomination afforded to common folk.

"You'll live like a queen," Stine promised her. "I'll only require you please myself." But to be placed on a pedestal merely for the purpose of being torn from it, night after night, was no better in Evelyn's estimation than the alley.

"Come." He led her into the adjoining room and positioned her in front of a full-length mirror. "The outdoors doesn't agree with you." He cited her tanned skin and rash of freckles. Then he gathered her shirt in back, drawing the cloth taut across her front. "See how you've lost weight?"

It had been awhile since Evelyn last faced her reflection. The naïve girl who ran from hardship and subsisted on the dream of a fairytale rescuer would be impressed and intimidated by the woman who replaced her. She saw wisdom in green eyes, determination in her posture, boldness in set lips. The new Evelyn Deveraux was disillusioned but stronger for it.

A few years ago, she would have jumped at an offer like this, at a man like Stine. Now the idea of shackling herself to such a benefactor was insufferable. Silas Kelly had ruined her for any man who sought to own her. The memory of the bandit prince was like the recollection of a trauma, poignant even repressed. He likely hadn't known the idea he'd planted, that she'd fallen in love with the life he presented.

Stine released her shirt, his hands wandering to her hips. Over Evelyn's shoulder, graphite-hued eyes devoured her image in the glass. He said, "I envy the man who won your virginity. Whatever the price, I would have outbid him." She tried to push his hands away, but his fingers dug in. "Don't take my proposal lightly," he warned. "I think I warrant your utmost consideration."

Released, Evelyn walked back through the French doors and out of the office. She clutched the banister with numb fingers, descended the stairs on shaky limbs that threatened to buckle with each step. She collected her Winchester and burst through the brothel doors. Closing her eyes, she lifted her face to the sun, willing the heat to melt the dread in her heart, to chase out the chill Stine had put into her bones. When she opened them again, sunspots loomed in her vision, and among them, she saw Malloy.

***

Trace stepped from the alley onto the boardwalk in front of The Old Mare and froze as the batwing doors parted and out strode Evelyn Deveraux. She stopped, stood with hair blazing red in the sunlight. He was close enough to see fear and sorrow on her face. He watched them fade, replaced by fury seemingly absorbed from the sun. He'd never seen a woman look so formidable.

She turned and faced him. For a few moments, she only blinked, as if he'd materialized out of thin air. Then she shifted, bringing the rifle up. Trace was so transfixed, he almost didn't react. Sluggish instincts didn't kick in until he was staring down the barrel from the wrong end. He dove for cover as the Winchester blasted away.

She worked the lever between shots to chamber the next round, not letting up until the gun was empty. Trace stuck his head around what remained of the building's corner in time to see her stow her weapon and mount up. Finally galvanized to action, he rushed for his own horse.

Evelyn spurred the sorrel to a gallop and steered it toward the edge of town, riding as fast as her ability would allow her to go and remain in the saddle. She risked a glance over her shoulder and spotted Malloy in pursuit. Either he had his horse nearby or commandeered one. On a whim, she tugged the reins and veered into an alley then onto a parallel street back into the center of Prospect. Over open terrain, Malloy would run her down. In town, he had a responsibility to safety that worked to her advantage. She zigzagged through the corridors of Prospect, dodging wagons and livestock, as pedestrians scrambled out of her path.

Pointing fingers and indignant shouts directed Trace as he followed Evelyn on her reckless escapade. She raced down one street only to double-back on another, running him in erratic circles and engulfing the frontier town in a storm of dust and chaos. Once, their vectors converged as she veered back onto Main Street yards ahead of him. He bore down on her, made a mad grab for her reins, her sleeve, anything. She evaded.

He glimpsed Casey a little ways down from the jail, trying to signal him. Trace made a wide sweeping gesture with one arm and hollered for him to keep on the walkway. A minute later, he heard the staccato crackle of rapid gunfire.

With an oath, Trace spun his horse around. He reached Main Street again, in time to see Evelyn fly past, hunched over her mount's neck, concentrating too hard to spare him a glance. Casey had holstered his six-gun and was aiming the Sharps taken from the jailhouse safe, aligning the barrel with the rider high-tailing it for open desert. Trace turned his horse into the line-of-fire, hauling back on the reins. His buckskin reared. Casey looked up in alarm.

"Sheriff, I might have shot you." The way his voice went high told Trace how close he'd come.

"I need her alive," croaked Trace. He looked over his shoulder at the line of churned-up dust stretching toward the horizon. His horse, burdened with his supplies in addition to his weight, was already in a lather, breathing like the bellows. Trace reckoned if Evelyn kept up her pace, she'd bake hers within ten miles.

7

The painted desert blurred like smeared chalk as the hot wind drew tears from Evelyn's eyes. Her horse's mane whipped her cheeks and her shirt rippled like a flag in a gale. She felt free.

Her mount slowed on its own, from a thundering gallop to a gliding canter to a weary trot. A glance over her shoulder showed Prospect shrunk to the size of a child's blocks. She'd gotten away.

As the rush of adrenaline faded and her pulse came down from its gallop, a peculiar tranquility came over Evelyn, dulling every sensation, blanketing her in disbelief. Had she really engaged the sheriff in a shootout then led him on a chase into the desert wilderness?

Coming across an arroyo, she hoped for water, but the creek bed was bone dry. She steered the sorrel into the wash and dismounted. Sweat evaporated, leaving woman and horse crusted with salt. Evelyn chugged her canteen though the contents were hot enough to brew tea. The gulch was deep enough to conceal her presence at a distance. Trembling with fatigue, she sank to the ground and leaned back against the gully wall, thankful for a sliver of shade.

She stared up at the butt of her rifle sticking out of the scabbard secured to the side of her horse. Her eyes narrowed as she focused on something above it. There was a nick in the leather. Her throat thickened as she realized it had been made by a bullet shot by Malloy's deputy and that he'd aimed for her.

As incredible as her most recent excursion into outlawry seemed, it struck Evelyn that her adventure had only begun. She was certain Malloy would be hunting her. The embarrassment of her initial escape would have been enough to earn his ire. Now that she'd shot at him and turned his town to bedlam, she could only imagine his wrath.

She hadn't planned it. Gunfire wasn't the method of engagement she would have chosen to preoccupy the lawman. She'd fled the bordello shaken and angry, not expecting to meet Malloy. She couldn't lash out at Stine, but the sheriff had presented a ready substitute. What would he do once he tracked her down? What would she do?

Wyatt seemed confident she could handle him. Evelyn wasn't so certain. The kiss through the cell bars had surely been a moment of weakness for the sheriff. She reckoned he wasn't a man to repeat his mistakes. Closing her eyes against the harsh desert glare, Evelyn returned to the dark jailhouse. She bit her lip as she recollected the grip of invisible hands on her hips, her bruising collision with hard iron bars—and hard male on the other side.

Evelyn had been kissed enough times to experience the whole spectrum from carefully chaste to mindless mauling. Hungry, possessive, and demanding, Trace's kiss held something new. She'd felt his frustration and sensed he wanted to resist but couldn't stop himself. She wondered if Mrs. Kelly had ever inspired such a response from him. Then it occurred to Evelyn the reason he'd tasted her at all was because he couldn't have Holly. He claimed the affair was finished, but she owed her escape to bottled tension and unrequited desire.

Her thoughts circled round the subject even as her mind grew muddled, until she fell asleep. In her dreams, she was back in Stine's office, but it was Malloy in the mirror, standing at her back. This time, the offer tempted her and so did the man behind it, behind her. Golden eyes gazed at her, reflecting in the glass. *You can have your own gun, Evelyn. But it won't protect you from me.* She gasped as the words—neither Stine's nor Malloy's—jolted her out of her dream.

***

Trace left his deputy to deal with the aftermath. As soon as it was confirmed nobody had been trampled or hit by one of Casey's bullets gone astray, he mounted the recovered buckskin, whistled for the hound to accompany him, and took off after Deveraux. The woman had a knack for slipping through his fingers, for getting beneath his skin. No way was he going to allow her to get away after the commotion she'd caused.

After a few miles riding at a steady, sustainable gait, his anger subsided, and he found himself shaking his head in bemused admiration. He'd never encountered a woman so impulsive, so spirited. He realized he didn't have a clue how to handle her and was looking forward to the challenge.

As the sun drifted westward, shadows condensed above the mountains to the southeast. Trace wondered what the storm would bring. Nothing cast the life-and-death struggle of desert existence into such sharp relief as the summer monsoons. Trace well-remembered the elemental fury that washed away Promise.

Only a long night of frantically bagging sand had saved the Malloy farm, five miles east and across the Gila River.

***

Evelyn opened her eyes to find the spotted dog from the jailhouse seated in front of her, tongue dangling out the side of its mouth. "What are you doing here?"

Cursing her unpreparedness, she drew her rifle then jammed an arm into her saddlebag in search of ammo. She wondered how many men Malloy had brought with him. "Where's your master?" She glanced up and down the gully while her fingers fumbled to stuff cartridges through the loading gate faster than coordination would allow. With five rounds in the bridge and as many fallen at her feet, she stole a glance over the edge. She saw one horse, which she recognized by its ebony mane and tail and hide the color of creamy butter. Nowhere did she see Malloy.

***

Trace slid into the gulch at a bend further down. Not a stealthy man, he had to pick his footing carefully. He wasn't going to give her the chance to blast away at him again. By the time he sighted his quarry, she was loading her gun, tipped off to his presence by the traitorous mutt. Trace crouched behind some rubble, waiting for his opportunity. When her attention went over the ledge, he made his move.

He rushed her, wagering that she was as poor a shot flustered as when caught unaware. She spotted him in her peripheral vision and turned toward him, raising the rifle. He closed the distance before she could level it. He tackled her, knocking the weapon from her grip, then scrambled to kick it away. Horse and hound shied from the skirmish. Trace used his advantage of strength and weight to wrestle her onto her belly and pin her with his body. Ready with rope, he wound and tied, his technique second nature after years as a cowhand in Texas. When he pushed to his feet, Evelyn was left trussed with wrists and ankles bound together behind her back.

***

Cheek to the ground, she let out a huff of indignation then coughed when she inhaled dust. She rolled her eyes upward, expecting to see smug satisfaction on his handsome face. Instead, he stooped to pick up her Winchester and collect the scattered cartridges. He plucked his hat, knocked from her head in the tussle, off the gully floor and tapped it against his thigh to shake loose the dust. He fetched his horse and led it down the embankment, then turned his attention to her sorrel.

Malloy ignored her, but the dog delighted in her predicament. It licked her face, causing her to sputter, and when she turned her head, it pawed her shoulder and prodded her with its snout. She fought to not laugh, until Malloy called it off.

While she was being tortured, he'd untacked her horse. She watched him drop her hat upside-down, twist the cap off one of his canteens, and drain it into the makeshift bowl. For the horse, she realized when he shot her an admonishing glare for neglecting the animal. The hound lapped up what little the sorrel didn't drink as Malloy proceeded to rub down the weary steed, speaking to it in a low, soothing tone, words intelligible from where she lay.

Evelyn's throat grew dry, her bindings pinched, her muscles cramped. She reckoned her discomfort was his way of paying her back. She gritted her teeth against it, until something skittering over the ground into her line-of-sight made her forget her pangs.

"Malloy?" He didn't answer. She didn't dare take her eyes off the scorpion. "Malloy," she said more urgently. She squirmed to scooch away from the critter then went rigid as it rotated toward her, stinger poised. She gulped a breath, ready to shriek when a boot stamped down in front of her face. Evelyn heard the exoskeleton crunch.

Trace crouched beside her, and Evelyn felt the tension holding her shoulders and thighs give way. He gripped her arm and hauled her to her knees then her feet. He worked the knot at her wrists, their positions too reminiscent of her dream for relief. As the coarse rope fell away, she felt cool metal graze her right wrist and heard a click. She raised her hand to gaze at the heavy double bracelet as he stepped around front of her. Before she knew it, he'd taken her left hand and locked the other iron loop, leaving her handcuffed.

He ordered her to sit, opened and handed her another canteen. The bindings made for an awkward grip, and water dribbled down her chin. She shot him an exasperated look. He dropped her hat into her lap and sitting opposite, tipped his down. He told her to rest up, that they'd ride once the horses recuperated.

***

Something bounced off Trace's hat with a hollow plop. He lifted his head, certain the woman was tossing pebbles at him. He hadn't meant to doze off. But Evelyn too had fallen asleep, elbows balanced on her knees, chin resting on the back of one hand still bound to the other.

Shade engulfed the arroyo, and the air was noticeably cooler. Trace peered up at the darkening sky and another raindrop splattered against his cheek. Pushing to his feet, he noticed water already trickled along the creek bed. He nudged Evelyn's boot with his toe. "Time to go. We have to get to higher ground."

She awoke with a groan and raised a hand to massage the crick in her neck, finding her reach encumbered by heavy iron manacles.

Already saddling the horses, he whistled for the dog that had wandered off. By the time he finished, a steady rain was falling and thunder rumbled. The hound returned, prancing through the puddles.

Trace directed Evelyn out of the gulch, occasionally aiding her climb with his hands on her hips, not wanting to take the time to free her. He commanded her and the dog to stay put then led his horse out before going back for hers.

By then, the creek was ankle deep. The sorrel, already made antsy by the weather, slipped on the muddy embankment and refused to give it a second attempt. Trace was forced to lead it upstream in search of a gentler incline. The water rose with every step and formed a current. He finally coaxed the mount back onto flat land a good quarter mile from where he'd left his prisoner and the other animals.

The sky opened up and water filled the wash in an instant, rushing from upstream, flowing in waterfalls over the banks. With a tight grip on the bridle, Trace led the horse parallel to the creek. Through the rain and dark, he struggled to make out his own horse, using its shape—head hung and rump to the wind—as a marker to judge his progress. It worried him that he could not yet see Evelyn. He feared she would use the opportunity to try to escape. When a flash of lightning revealed her figure, the flood of relief surprised him. Though she vanished the next instant, he fixated on the spot, waiting for the next illuminating bolt.

***

Evelyn squinted through the downpour, watching the raging waters rise, afraid she'd see man and horse sweep past her. Webs of purple lightning flashed and crackled across the sky. Squatting beside the dog, she stroked its wet fur compulsively, more to soothe herself than the mutt.

The next strike was exceptionally bright and left her temporarily blinded. She couldn't see the animals beside her. Disorientated, she rocked back off her heels and landed on her butt in a puddle. Rain pelted her hat, as loud to her ears as the current crashing through the arroyo. Not wanting to be stamped upon should the buckskin spook, Evelyn shifted onto her knees then staggered to her feet.

The darkness blinded her as effectively as the lightning. The overwhelming noise deafened her. Deprived of her senses, she stumbled and pitched forward.

***

Trace paused, waiting to recover his sight. On the wind, he thought he heard a scream. Then the dog started barking. As his vision returned, he expected to see it bounding toward him. Almost to his horse, he looked for Evelyn, scanning every which way when the storm gave him light. She was nowhere to be seen.

The hound continued to bark at the water, its paws planted near the edge where chunks of embankment were dropping into the current. Trace shouted at it to come away. Ignoring him, the hound suddenly gave chase, bolting along the bank. It hit him like a punch to the gut—Trace knew what had become of Evelyn. He lunged for his horse, swung into the saddle, and dug in his heels.

Pacing the hound, he searched the churning mud, unable to make out what the dog saw, unable to lasso what he couldn't see. So, he urged the buckskin to race ahead, hoping for a bottleneck in the gulch. He saw a bend in the creek, brown foam indicating shallower waters, and decided it was his best bet.

He vaulted from the saddle and hurried to ready his rope. He frantically worked hands into wet leather gloves as the dog sprinted toward him. Trace shoved the coil over his head and shoulders and slid down the bank. Two strides into the turbulent stormwaters, a body collided with his.

Trace threw both arms around the form as the rope cinched about his torso, going taut between him and where it looped around the saddle horn. He fought for his footing and he fought to hang on as the water eroded soil beneath his boots and the current threatened to wrest the woman from his hold. Evelyn's hands, trapped in cuffs, clawed at him, failing to latch on.

She was undermining his balance. He needed her on his back, but changing positions was too risky. If he lost his grip, she'd be swept away. If he lost his footing, they both might drown at the end of the rope.

Letting the current press her against him, Trace lifted her arms over and behind his head, felt the manacles gouge his neck. He looped an arm around her waist and hooked the other under her knee, hoisting her leg up over his hip. He switched arms and together, they fought for balance against the current, until her legs were wound around him, above the water. Trace reached behind her for the rope, praying it and the saddle and the horse all stayed put.

Hand over hand, one shuffled step at a time, Trace moved toward the bank, the barking dog egging him on. Mud filled his boots, fire filled his lungs, the rope sawed his flesh. Evelyn's thighs were clamped around his hips. Her fingers clutched his hair and collar. He gritted his teeth and pushed through the pain.

Finally, they were out. Trace pitched forward onto his knees and elbows, panting for breath, quaking with fatigue. Cool rain pummeled his back, streamed into his eyes. Beneath him, Evelyn's strength dissolved. Her limbs went limp and she began to shiver. Even with Trace's body sheltering hers, her teeth chattered. For a while, shaking was the only movement either could muster.

Eventually, Trace worked the lasso back over his shoulders and head. When his hands steadied enough, he produced a key and unshackled his prisoner. Evelyn swiped at her cheeks, wiping away mud, rainwater, maybe tears.

The monsoon moved on as they lay recuperating. An orange glow in the west condensed into a line of fire on the horizon as the setting sun revealed itself beneath the ceiling of storm clouds. It occurred to Trace that he ought to use the dregs of daylight to find shelter. But he was too preoccupied with the woman he'd almost let drown, who whimpered whenever he shifted away.

He gathered her up off the ground, onto his lap, alternately rubbing her arms and back to warm her, finally pulling her to his chest. He assured her she was going to be all right. He told himself he owed her this, that it was the least he could do.

So, they huddled with fading light reflecting off their faces, in their eyes.

8

Evelyn didn't want to wake. A heavy warmth lay over her body, pressing her to a firm bed, holding her near the edge of consciousness so she drifted in and out. A pleasant scent surrounded her, earthy creosote mingled with smoke and a hint of wet fur. She wished to remain nestled in drowsy sanctuary, but her bladder was full.

With a sigh, she squirmed out from under a pile of coverings that included bedrolls, saddle blankets, and spare clothing. Some of the items were dusted in ash as though they'd been dried over a campfire. She found herself in a shallow cave, with no memory of how she came there. Her clothes were damp, and her boots were nowhere to be seen.

She stood, wincing at the first touch of cool stone beneath her bare feet. Her knees trembled to support her weight, as if she were rising after a long illness. Every muscle in her body ached. She stooped to pick up a blanket and draped it over her shoulders. She remembered being cold, feeling she'd never be warm again. She padded over the rock floor toward the cave's mouth. Outside, the sun was bright, the morning air clear. Evelyn was brought up short by the sight of the man sitting just beyond the entrance, naked from the waist up.

An angry red line cut diagonal across his tanned, muscular back. His hair, every shade of blond with some brown mixed in, wasn't long enough to conceal the raw skin at the top of his spine. The memory struck her—of being swept away and rescued. Trace Malloy had fought for her life, risked his own. Why?

She fixated on the spattering of freckles atop his shoulders, felt an unnerving urge to trace them with her fingertips. The mottled dog beside him detected her presence and hopped up to greet her with wagging tail. Malloy twisted to look over his shoulder. Seeing her, he rose, though with greater effort than the hound. Keen eyes looked her up and down before focusing on her face. Finding the golden gaze too intense, she cast her eyes downward, over his broad chest to their unshod feet. She didn't know why it should strike her as intimate, standing toe to toe with him in such dishevel.

He took her hand, slid her sleeve up her arm to reveal one bruised and chaffed wrist. It perplexed her that coarse hands could be so gentle. She studied his solemn expression, felt a confusing compulsion to brush the tawny hair from his forehead, to lean into his chest and experience his embrace once more. He reached for her other hand, but she pulled it back and gestured to some indistinct location to the right. "I need to…"

He acknowledged her meaning with a nod but didn't release her when she made to step away. "There's a patch of cholla cactus over yonder," he said. "I suggest the other way." She bobbed her head, and he let her go.

Once her business was done, Evelyn took a seat on a sun-warmed rock. Her view was that of the hillside sloping down to the flat rangelands below. Patches of sage and cactus grew in the gaps between granite boulders. She could pick out no easy path down the incline and wondered how Malloy had managed the climb in the dark, leading two horses. He must have been exhausted upon reaching the cave, but rather than seek his own rest, he'd tended to her comfort.

She reached up to comb back a strand of hair only to catch her fingers in a tangle. She must look a fright. But her physical appearance didn't worry her as much as what else Malloy's penetrating gaze might discern. It wasn't just her body that was raw. She felt exposed by the ordeal, knew there was no state so vulnerable as fear.

They were enemies, lawman and lady outlaw. Yet, after dragging her from danger, he'd held her, had spoken to ease her panic. She hadn't been able to make out his words in the rain, but she'd seemed to hear them throughout her dreams. Had he stayed close to her during the night? Watched over her?

***

Trace donned his shirt and hat before she returned to camp. He hauled out the makeshift bed he'd fashioned for her and sorted the items, stuffing spare clothing back into his saddlebags. He considered a moment before folding his badge up in his vest and stowing it as well. Their boots were propped upside-down with sticks over the coals of a fire. He'd swapped the ammo in his gun and cartridge belt for new, dry rounds. When Evelyn returned, he tossed her a pair of socks. He said, "I couldn't find your hat."

"I ought to thank you," she began, obviously reluctant to express her gratitude.

He spared her with a shake of his head. "It was my fault." She watched him pull on his socks and boots and wondered when he'd become angry.

"I'm the one who fell in—"

"You're my responsibility," he said. His prisoner and he'd almost gotten her killed, thought Trace. If he wanted her cooperation, he needed to convince her that he was capable of protecting her against retaliation from Hennessy and Stine. Instead, he'd put her in danger. He needed time to gain her trust, to show her she had options. An idea occurred to him. "Are you hungry?"

Evelyn's stomach grumbled at the promise of food but turned at the prospect of trail rations. She shrugged.

"I know a place sure to have a home-cooked spread." He raised his eyebrows in question.

"Throw in a hot bath and it's a deal," she said.

He pursed his lips. "I can't guarantee it'll be hot."

He readied the horses while she pulled on her socks and boots. They mounted up and headed out, dog leading the way along a deer trail that zigzagged down the hillside.

The desert heat came on as if the storm never happened, the sun baking away all evidence. Evelyn's damp clothing grew hot and stiff, causing her to sweat and itch. When they passed the arroyo, the floodwaters were gone, only a creamy silt left behind. The storm had brought a fleeting energy, a touch of life and death, to a forgetting landscape.

***

Trace led Evelyn northwest, away from the hills, until they met and crossed the Gila River, then west along its northern bank.

"So, where are we going?" she asked, bringing the sorrel alongside his buckskin. He glanced sidelong at her and didn't answer right away.

"Home," he finally said as the blue farmhouse came into view. Moving around some trees at the river's edge, he turned to voice a stipulation. "Don't mention Silas Kelly," he warned.

"Why would I mention…" Her words stalled.

Trace looked forward and saw what drew her attention. He brought his mount to a stop with a hoarse, "Whoa."

The swimming hole, made from a rock dam downstream, was occupied. A man and woman stood waist-deep in the pool, holding one another in a naked embrace.

Water droplets adorned the woman's brown hair wound into a bun. Her eyes were closed, head fallen back, exposing her throat to the man's lips as he held her against him with hand splayed over her back. His other hand rested between her breasts. The man had the same sandy hair and brawny build as the sheriff. He raised hazel-green eyes to them as his mouth left the lady's skin.

"Uh, howdy," he said after a beat, alerting the woman who opened her eyes and let out a surprised "Oh." She ducked behind the man as he turned to face the visitors.

For a moment, Evelyn couldn't help but stare at the man's chest covered in rough scars. The dog launched itself off the bank to paddle circles around the couple.

"Good to see you, Trace," the man said. Despite their timing, the surprise seemed welcome. Huddled behind him, cheeks rouged with embarrassment now more than passion, the lady quietly echoed the greeting. "Get caught in the storm?" The man looked back and forth between Trace and Evelyn.

"It's been a long night," said Trace after calling the dog back to shore. "We were hoping to bum breakfast."

"Sure." A cough interrupted the response. As the man gruffly cleared his throat, Evelyn noticed the woman's chocolate-colored eyes sparkled with mischief, her hands invisible beneath the water. She suppressed a smile and glanced at Trace to see whether he struggled to do the same. But the sheriff's expression was solemn.

The man told them leftovers could be found in the kitchen. With a nod, Trace directed his horse toward the house. Evelyn followed but stole a glance back over her shoulder in time to see the man turn and pounce and the lovers submerge.

They situated their mounts in a corral around front of the farmhouse and worked in silence to unburden the horses while the hound sniffed about the perimeter. Evelyn wondered what about the encounter caused Malloy to knit his brow and clench his jaw. Surely, he didn't have a history with this woman as well. She managed to drag her saddle off the sorrel's back and lug it over to the fence. When Trace turned to take it from her, she asked, "What happened to him?" She watched a wave of pain wash over his features before they hardened.

"Kelly men shot him." He jerked the saddle from her hands and heaved it atop the mesquite rail before brushing past her to finish untacking his ride. They draped the saddle blankets over the fence and hung headgear on posts, then Evelyn trailed Trace to the gate. With his hands on the latch, he stopped and turned to her. "He's my brother." Evelyn nodded, having guessed as much. "It should have been me."

9

Trace left Evelyn standing at the corral gate. She was still puzzling over his declaration and the guilt that accompanied it when he gained the steps to the wraparound porch. As he disappeared inside, she spied movement in a second-story window. A curtain fell back into place as if someone had been peering out, watching them. She might have dismissed it, except the dog saw too. It perked up its ears, let out a yip, and bounded inside. Evelyn eyed the veil a moment longer, to see whether the voyeur reappeared. When she headed inside, the hound was nowhere to be seen. Movement in the kitchen drew her attention to the left.

Trace waved her toward a large, sturdy table. She sat and watched him move about with easy familiarity. "Is it typical for a lawman to serve his prisoner breakfast?"

"Just for today, let's consider you a guest." He dropped a plate laden with ham, potatoes, and eggs in front of her.

"A truce?"

"A chance to establish some common ground," he said, sitting across from her with his own plate, removing his hat and setting it beside him.

"To what end?" He shrugged. She glanced around the kitchen, bigger than the one-room sod house where she grew up. "So, this is home?" He told her that his grandparents settled there, that his father had taught him and his brother to farm. "Yet you became sheriff."

"Tyler always wanted to take over the land," he said. "I didn't like having my path laid before me." She expected him to ask her story, how she'd come to Prospect. Truth was, she hadn't liked the path before her any more than he had. But he didn't ask, so in awkward silence, they ate.

Their meal was interrupted by a peel of laughter as the dog trotted into the room. A tow-headed child was tugged off balance as he toddled behind clutching its tail. The boy let go and after a wide, blue-eyed gander at Evelyn, sped over to Trace. He took ahold of the sheriff's trousers and pulled himself on tiptoes in an obvious plea to be picked up.

Rather than oblige, Trace looked to the small-statured woman who appeared in the doorway. Her hair was only a shade darker than that of the child, her eyes silver-lining gray. Evelyn didn't know if her patient smile was for the man or the boy. She entered the kitchen long enough to take a couple biscuits from the bread box and some cubes of sugar from a jar on the window sill. She called for the child to follow her.

When the toddler reached for the hat on the tabletop, Trace blocked him. "Mind your ma," he ordered.

The woman's composure didn't falter. Gayly, she called again. "Shall we visit Belle?" The boy made a high-pitched imitation of a horse's neigh and scurried to follow her.

As Trace scowled after the mother and son, Evelyn said, "What's your beef with the boy?"

"My sister has been through enough," he said. "She doesn't need any more grief."

Evelyn took a big bite rather than annoy him further.

***

They'd just finished eating when the couple from the river, now clothed, joined them in the kitchen. Evelyn mumbled thanks as the woman collected their plates and forks.

"Today ain't Sunday," Trace said to the man. It was the same admonishment their father would use when he found the brothers taking a swim break from their chores.

"Was working at making a couple of farmhands, if we could get some privacy." The other man winked.

The woman's cheeks went pink in the middle of refilling their cups with coffee. If she noticed the talk didn't affect Evelyn, she didn't let on. "The river's free if you fancy a bath," she said. "I have clothes you can borrow. My name is Beth, by the way. This is my husband, Tyler."

"Evelyn Deveraux, much obliged."

Beth went upstairs and returned with a stack of clothing and some toiletries. Evelyn stood and, when the sheriff didn't object, followed her out the back door.

Tyler took Evelyn's seat, sipped the abandoned coffee, and waited to hear the story behind the visit.

"She rides with Hennessy," said Trace. "They ambushed the stage. Jerrod Kelly was riding shotgun, was hurt bad. I'm hoping she'll tell me where to find the rest of them."

"He going to pull through?" Tyler's teasing turned to concern. "How's Holly holding up?"

"I reckon he will." Trace rolled his shoulders, stretching sore muscles. "I promised her justice."

"So, you gave her another reason to worry."

Trace scowled. "It's my duty."

"What makes you think the lady will cooperate?"

"When Hennessy don't come for her, she'll realize what kind of man he is," said Trace.

"Who says he ain't coming?" Trace gave him a tired look. The spotted hound made another pass through the kitchen, stopping to greet Tyler. It sat back on its haunches, leaning against his knee to receive a vigorous belly rub. "You got a woman yet?" Tyler asked. "One that ain't a prisoner?"

"I get one when I need one." He knew that wasn't what his brother meant. "To tell the truth, I've met none that holds that appeal." He rubbed eyes scratchy from sitting over a campfire all night as he kept swapping out and reheating Evelyn's blankets.

"You're looking for one that matches your office when you ought to be after the one that matches you."

"Being sheriff means more to me than finding the right woman," said Trace, "or I would have married Holly." He ran a hand over the tabletop, marveled at how it held up to generations of use.

"What does it mean to you, Trace?"

He sighed. Tyler's interrogation and the itch of dirty clothing were the only things keeping him from dozing off where he sat. "Town needs an honest man in office." It was an old excuse, his answer to a tired debate.

"You sure you don't aim to please the dead? Ma and Pa would have been proud regardless. And you don't owe Del Cooper a thing."

Trace stood. "I'm going to take a nap," he said. "Wake me when they're done."

"Trace." He paused in the doorway, let his brother have the final word, too exhausted to keep up the argument. Tyler said, "Maybe Holly wasn't the one after all."

***

Evelyn shed her clothes at the river's edge and stood for a minute in the shallows, cool silt rising between her toes, sun's kiss bringing a blush to her skin. When she sank into the pool, water rushed over her like a liquid breeze, more refreshing than any bath in a zinc tub. The soap stung but the river soothed her chaffed wrists and other scrapes inflicted by the flood's violence. She drifted in the water, let her hair float on the current, and felt renewed.

Living out of a saddlebag, riding with a rugged bunch of men, gave little opportunity for matters of hygiene and no privacy. While her confederates' foremost priority upon entering a town was to locate a saloon, Evelyn's first stop was the bath house. Yet trail dust and the sweat of a long ride didn't disgust her, not after the filth of her previous occupation.

Patrons of The Treasure Room were assured the girl presented for their entertainment was fresh just for them. The reality of that claim meant Evelyn had to wait her turn for a quick dip in a tepid tub contaminated with the residues of fornication and too much perfume before receiving an application of powder and donning her costume for the next gentleman's pleasure. The

Old Mare, pre-Easton Stine, offered only a basin and cloth to swab juices from her flesh before accepting the next drunk into her bed.

Across the river, wildflowers swayed in a gentle breeze. The sky was a crisp blue. She wanted to believe the Gila could purify her soul as perfectly as its waters swept the grit and suds from her body.

While Evelyn scrubbed dirt from her pores and mud from her hair, Beth gathered the garments left on shore and perched on a rock downstream to wash them.

"You don't have to do that." Beth said that she didn't mind and carried on, so Evelyn turned her eyes from the memory-evoking chore. Her mother had worked hunched over a washboard, day in and day out, until her knuckles reddened, her skin cracked, and her hands cramped so that the joy of brushing her daughter's hair became a torment. Evelyn dreaded the slow effect of physical labor. Beth seemed to endure it well. It made her curious. She asked, "Do you enjoy this living?"

Intelligent, brown eyes focused on Evelyn. Beth seemed to consider the inquirer more than the question, the explanation more than the answer. "Tyler and I are building a life for ourselves, with our own hands," she said. "Teamwork makes the burden lighter, the rewards sweeter. Yes, I enjoy it."

She probably wouldn't understand why Evelyn had run from such a life or her motivations for choosing the one she did. "How did you meet?" She expected Beth to reply with something conventional, like a church social or country dance.

Instead, she said, "I tended to his wounds."

She nursed him after he was shot. Evelyn knew why Trace had told her not to mention Silas Kelly. "That must have been awful," she muttered, expecting the conversation to end there.

But after some hesitation, Beth said, "It had been a long time since I'd felt useful, felt seen." Evelyn sensed something private and painful underlying her words. "Tyler made me feel worthy again. We healed each other."

***

Trace lugged his saddlebag upstairs, to one of the six bedrooms. He wanted to collapse upon the bed and into sleep, but he was filthy. Beth kept the farmhouse so tidy that he'd feel guilty soiling the clean sheets. A bath in the river sounded divine, but he had to make do with a basin and pitcher of water. He eased out of his boots and shrugged off his shirt, starting a pile on the floor. He coiled his gun-belt and set it on the dresser. Then he peeled down the top half of his underwear, letting the union suit hang from his waist.

He washed his face first, then sponged the sweat and dirt from his torso, as best he could reach. Beth put new curtains in the windows when she and Tyler moved to the farm. Trace stared at them until he recalled the view they hid, of the fields behind the house and beyond. He left the washrag floating in the basin and reached for the window covering, resisting the compulsion to sweep it aside, only parting it a slit. He sucked in a breath at the sight of Evelyn standing naked on the riverbank.

Her hair hung like a cape down her back. Long, milky limbs could have been the model for the nude painting at The Old Mare. When she splashed into the pool, Trace's mouth went dry with a powerful thirst he reckoned could only be slated by drinking the water off her skin. When she tipped back her head to rinse the auburn mane, the curtain fell from trembling fingers.

He'd begun to sweat again, heart loping, itching skin prompting him to remove the rest of his clothing. He worked mud-stiffened trousers down muscular legs and finished shedding the union suit. He held the washrag spread over one hand over the basin, pouring fresh water onto it, again and again as he swathed fevered skin. He attempted to balance thoroughness with a ginger touch as he bathed the sensitive flesh of his groin, as his cock began to swell with desires he struggled to repress. He left the temptation of the window and lay on the bed to air dry.

Trace closed his eyes and her image filled his mind, faithful to all the details gleaned through the slit in the curtain. He envisioned them on the riverbank together. Evelyn was above him, straddling his hips, skin glistening with water, wet auburn hair plastered to her body, with the sun blazing behind her. He could almost smell the grass, almost feel the mud squish beneath him. His cock was convinced she was real. It went hard so fast Trace felt light-headed. He told himself his reaction was ridiculous, that he'd been too long without a woman. He resisted the urge to take himself in hand, instead took fistfuls of the quilt at his sides. She swayed above him. His hips rose to meet her. He imagined her head falling back in ecstasy and groaned. He fell asleep still yearning for her phantom body.

When he woke, his skin was dry and cool, the consuming fantasy a residual ache in his balls. He dressed in spare clothes that he kept in the dresser for occasions when he stayed over at the farm. He rooted in his saddlebag for his badge and pinned it in place with a promise not to forget his purpose again.

He'd napped too long. Beth was in the kitchen starting supper. He found Tyler on the porch, sitting in their pa's old rocker. He nodded toward the hillside. The buckskin and sorrel had been turned out to graze along with a white filly. Evelyn helped Aimee gather wildflowers, wearing a dress that belonged to Beth. Oddly, the sight made him ache in entirely new places.

"I asked you to wake me," Trace grumbled.

"Reckoned you could use the sleep," said Tyler. "Sounds like you had a hell of a night."

"What did she say?" Trace tried to sound indifferent.

"Only that you had to fish her out of some rough waters."

"It was a might bit more heroic than that," said Trace. He continued to scowl at the vixen putting nature's beauty to shame. She was wearing his hat again.

"She cleans up nice," his brother commented.

"She's trouble," said Trace.

Tyler grinned. "You watched from the window, didn't you?"

10

Evelyn watched Trace emerge from the house and stand awhile beside his brother before stepping to the edge of the porch and raising his hand to shade his eyes. He scrutinized her, no doubt concerned for his sister, afraid she'd say something to shock the young mother. He'd be relieved to know there'd been little conversation. They'd shared only a few amused smiles as the boy dictated which flowers they picked, pointing and oohing at each selection, or played hide-and-seek, popping up out of the swaying grasses and giggling as they feigned surprise.

"How do you know my brother?" Evelyn turned to find gray eyes regarding her with curiosity.

"I spent a few hours in his jail." She omitted what had transpired during her incarceration. "I expect he means to lock me back up and throw away the key, for all the trouble I've caused him."

Aimee smiled. "Rescuing a lady in distress is a welcome trouble for a man if ever there was one." The smile dimmed. "And if he locks you up, it'll be to keep you safe."

"I'd escape," said Evelyn.

"Good. Perhaps you can free him as well."

It wasn't the reply Evelyn expected. It prompted her to ask, "Who's the father?" The other woman hesitated to answer.

Eventually, Aimee said, "All my life, people have sought to confine me. My parents wanted to preserve my health. My brothers wished to protect my virtue. To my first husband, I was a prize to be kept, political currency to further his career. Josiah—Josiah's father— set me free. He took me on an adventure, taught me passion, gave me a taste of life unfettered. When I thought him gone, I learned he'd left me with child—a reminder of his love, a reason to survive."

The boy led the way, up the hill to a lone tree atop the ridge. When Evelyn saw the wooden crosses, she knew why they'd been picking wildflowers. Aimee cleared away the old tributes, while her son toddled in her wake, placing a new flower upon each grave. A row of four were all carved with the name Malloy.

Then Aimee moved around the tree to a marker set apart from the others. She settled down in front of it and placed one flower at a time as the child handed each to her, until there were no more. When mother and son had paid their respects, they headed back down the hill, hand in hand. Only then did Evelyn satisfy her curiosity.

The name on the cross was Josiah Wyland. There were no dates, but Evelyn knew the day he'd died. She'd witnessed the fatal shot. Two other men had expired in Prospect that day. One of them was Silas Kelly.

Evelyn saw Trace start up the ridge, passing his sister and nephew on their way down. She waited as he came to stand beside her. "Were they friends?" she asked, remembering that Silas's last words were for Wyland.

The sheriff shrugged. "They were cut from the same cloth."

Evelyn studied the flowers that adorned the gunfighter's grave. She thought of the bandit prince who found his peace not in love but in pain, whose grave she'd never visited. "No." She glanced down the hill, at the woman and boy walking together back to the farmhouse. She shook her head. "They weren't."

Trace reckoned if he wanted her cooperation, it was time they talked. Deciding that a compliment was a sound strategy to steer the conversation away from dead gunmen, he said what had been on his mind heading up the hill. "That dress sure suits you."

"You mean it suits you." He cocked his head, blinked. She gestured to the wooden cross. "He married your sister, but you wouldn't allow him to be buried alongside your kin."

Trace scowled. "What's Wyland got to do with it?"

"That badge doesn't make you just any more than this dress makes me respectable," she said. "What happens when I take it off, who am I then?" His mouth gaped, offense undermined by the idea of the dress slipping from her body. She put her hand on his chest, covering his star. "Who are you now, Trace? Why did you bring me here?"

"I wanted to give you a choice." He swallowed the lump in his throat. "You're not the type for outlawry," he said. "Maybe you're not the type for whoring either. But there are options between the two." She shook her head, but he pressed on. "Tell me what Hennessy's planning and who all's involved. Let me help you."

"I already made my choice," she said, a hint of uncertainty in her voice that he attributed to fear of repercussions.

"I can protect you," he promised.

"Like you protected your brother and sister?" He flinched at her words and his hands clenched, but his expression remained earnest. She felt his heart thud under her palm. "Where does your responsibility end, Trace?"

He was struck by the shine in her eyes, confused by her melancholy tone. "What do you want?"

At that instant, Evelyn didn't know the answer. Perhaps she wanted what Aimee had lost. The moment was interrupted by the ringing of the porch bell bidding them to supper. Tyler had lifted his nephew up to make the summons.

They led the horses into the barn and secured the animals in stalls, not a word passing between them. Trace took his hat from her head and broke the silence. "I'm taking you back to Prospect tomorrow. You can come as my witness or my prisoner."

***

Supper was a quiet affair. Evelyn seemed lost in her thoughts. Trace watched her as if he could read them. The others focused on the business of eating, sensitive to their guests' moods, making whispered requests to pass butter or greens and mumbling thanks. Aimee softly admonished the boy for passing morsels to the hound who'd positioned itself under his chair.

Trace imagined Evelyn dwelling on the condition of betraying her lover or facing prison. He wanted to tell her Wyatt Hennessy wouldn't hesitate to save his own skin if their positions were reversed. But he reckoned it was best not to press or pry, that the conviction would be stronger if she came to it on her own. Waiting was not his strong suit. It took a pointed look from Tyler for him to recognize that the tapping that filled the stillness was his own toe.

When Wyatt assigned her to deal with the sheriff, Evelyn hadn't dreamed she'd be eating supper with Malloy's family. She could imagine her boss's amused praise, but she couldn't take credit for how events had progressed. Chance swept her from one situation to another. In the midst of the storm, she had no influence on the current. The truce was almost up. Whatever game this was would resume once they left the farmhouse. Malloy had called her out with his ultimatum. She didn't know her next move, only that she couldn't let him take her back to Prospect.

"Where do you come from, Evelyn?" Beth interrupted her musings. "Do you have people in the territory?" All eyes focused on Evelyn, none so intent as the sheriff's.

Before she could answer, Aimee chimed in. "Or did you come from the east like our friend Holly?" At the name, Evelyn caught the golden gaze and it was Trace's turn to evade.

Tyler drew her attention with a comment of his own. "If you grew up in these parts, you'd be familiar with the old town of Promise. We might all have been neighbors without knowing it." He smiled at his wife. "Until our paths cross, one day."

"I'm afraid I don't know Promise," Evelyn lied, remembering her mission. "The place I grew up was too small to even have a name." That much was truth. "I doubt it's there anymore." She couldn't decide if Trace seemed suspicious as he asked which town had been nearest. "Tucson," she answered, another lie.

***

Mother and son were the first to retire. Beth went up with them to ready a room for Evelyn. Left to wander the parlor, she stopped to study the framed portraits arranged on the mantle.

There was a severe mustachioed man beside a boy a few years older than Aimee's son. Evelyn looked to Trace, loitering in the hall, for an explanation. He told her the man was Del Cooper, Beth's father, buried with his son at their old cabin. Another frame held a childhood picture of the Malloy brothers and sister. The boys looked hearty with sun-bleached hair while Aimee appeared pale and waifish. Josiah Wyland's image was absent, but Evelyn recognized another. "Your deputy's portrait is on the mantle," she said, raising an eyebrow at the sheriff. He explained that Casey was courting Aimee. "I reckon he's not having much success."

His eyes narrowed at her smirk. "He's a good man."

Evelyn shook her head, remembering the tongue-tied tenderfoot who'd ogled her at the jailhouse. "He isn't dangerous enough."

She felt her heartbeat begin to skip as Trace stepped near. He said, "Danger isn't what she needs."

"Maybe not," said Evelyn with a coy smile, "but if he stood a chance, his likeness would be upstairs on her dresser, not down here next to ma and pa."

Beth announced that their rooms were ready. Trace escorted her upstairs, down a dark hall. There were six bedrooms, three at the front and three at the back of the house. Candlelight illuminated two opposite rooms. Trace waved the hound toward the one that was his for the night. He turned to Evelyn, wanting her decision but refusing to ask for it. She seemed softer shrouded in shadow. He reckoned it was part of her allure but couldn't deny the effect. He wanted to lie her down, craved her compliant beneath him, malleable to his will, to his strength. "Until tomorrow," he said, thickly.

Inside her room, Evelyn leaned back against the closed door and breathed a sigh of relief. Her body was trying to betray her. She'd never craved a man before, yet each encounter with Malloy further awakened some primal, persuasive call to submit. She feared their proximity was increasingly jeopardous to her mission, her freedom, ultimately her heart.

Looking in the mirror, she didn't recognize herself. The heat radiating from her core brought a rosy flush to her neck and cheeks. Her eyes dilated with the desire that pulsed in sensual places. She blamed the dress, the way the skirt swished about her limbs while leaving her inner thighs vulnerable to sensation. She was glad to find her clothes, cleaned and dried, lay folded upon the bed. But as she rid herself of the borrowed garment, exposure only magnified her arousal. She wondered, if she went to Malloy, would he accommodate her need to be filled or would he shun her, would moral superiority be the basis of his rejection or would he find her inadequate to substitute the coveted Mrs. Kelly? No way would she lower herself to find out.

She changed back into the man's shirt and trousers, feeling resolve return. Though coarse material still bothered swollen flesh, she found she could banish the physical ache. But another kind of emptiness lingered. This place, the welcoming people, had disarmed her. She felt tempted to confide in his family, to give herself over to the promise of his protection. She told herself it would only last until he got his man.

***

Evelyn dozed, knowing that nerves would awaken her periodically, knowing he would have to sleep eventually. It was dark when she slipped out of bed. She lit the bedside candle and sat for a minute, listening to the silence of the house, a blanket she'd found draped over a chair pulled around her shoulders.

She tiptoed across the hall in stocking feet, cringing at every creak of the floorboards, and peered through the cracked door. Trace slouched in a still rocker, his arms crossed over his chest. The spotted hound lay curled at his feet. Evelyn carried her boots, setting them on the undisturbed bed before creeping closer to the slumbering sheriff. She half-expected him to open his eyes at any moment. She leaned over him and her hair tumbled over her shoulder, brushing his cheek.

"You awake, Malloy?" she whispered. "I've made my decision." She could feel his breath against her lips. She wondered what he'd do if he awoke and caught her. She wondered what she was supposed to do if he didn't. She touched her lips to his.

He mumbled, "Holly."

Evelyn froze, waiting for him to recognize his mistake. His chest rose and fell in regular cadence. He slept on. She left the blanket, spreading it over his chest and backing away. The hound lifted its head and whined when she slid the window open. She collected her boots and climbed through, having decided the farmhouse probably had a hundred creaky floorboards, any one of which might betray her. She pulled on her boots and dropped off the roof onto the soft soil of the field, then dashed to the barn. Humiliation quickly burned away the shock of hearing the other woman's name. She saddled her sorrel, cursing the tightness in her breast, the stinging of her eyes. She rode off, wanting escape.

11

The night air smelled of rain. A cool breeze wafted through the open window, causing the curtain to float, contributing to the chill in the room, awakening Trace. He discovered he'd fallen asleep in the rocker. A warm weight anchored his feet to the floor, and the hound's soft snore reached his ears. He adjusted the blanket in his lap, tugging it up to his chin. This time, the scent of gardenia pulled him out of sleep. He lifted the blanket to his nose, puzzled at the familiar perfume. A narrow vertical line of flickering light distracted him from the coverlet. He'd left the door to his room open. The one across the hall was also ajar, the glow coming from Evelyn's room.

Trace surged to his feet, startling the dog and causing the chair to rock. He balled up the blanket, tossing it into the seat, and stalked toward the light which seemed to tremble and shrink at his approach. He crossed the hall in two strides, swept open the door, and barged in… on no one. The borrowed dress lay across an empty bed. A candle had been left burning, slowly drowning in a pool of molten wax. It quivered in the wind created by Trace's intrusion and fizzled out. The clicking of canine toenails upon the wood floor followed him into the room. "Some guard dog you are," he admonished the hound.

As Trace moved down the hall toward the stairs, the floorboards heralded his every step. He let out a hiss of disgust for having slept through Evelyn's departure. He stopped outside Aimee's room, opening the door enough for the lean mutt to squeeze through. He watched it hop onto the bed and turn around three times before settling into position for a comfortable sleep.

Trace crept downstairs, trying unsuccessfully to mute his movement. He checked the kitchen and parlor, standing in each room long enough for his eyes to adjust. He imagined her restless, wandering the house whilst wrestling with the choice he'd put before her. He hoped to find her sitting in quiet contemplation, but the furniture was all deserted. He ventured out onto the porch, thinking that maybe she'd needed some air. The tree on the ridge was a dark blot against the charcoal clouds, the hillside a uniform blackness. He marched to the barn, noting as he drew near that light leaked from the cracks between boards. He found a lantern left burning. The sorrel was gone. "Reckon you have your answer," he said aloud.

He readied his horse, cursing himself for expecting a woman to choose reason over fancy. If she meant to rendezvous with Hennessy, she was making a mistake. A man like that would lead her to ruin then leave her. The thought reminded him he needed to have a talk with Aimee about accepting Casey Horne.

He led the buckskin from the barn then realized he didn't know which direction she'd gone. If he waited, the dawn might reveal some sign of her, or the rain might come and erase it. If he waited, hours would be added to her head start. Trace didn't want to wait, he didn't want to explain to Tyler how his prisoner had stolen away in the night, and he didn't want to return to Prospect empty-handed. He knew he might search every town in the county and still not find her, so he decided to follow his original plan and ride for Tucson. Maybe she still had kin in that area.

He headed southeast over open desert, met the stage road and followed it south. When the rain started, he pulled the long oilcloth duster from his saddlebag and pushed through it. If Evelyn was headed the same direction, he intended to catch up. He only hoped she kept to the trail rather than risk getting lost in the wilderness. He doubted a former prostitute would know much about desert survival. Exposure was a constant danger, and summer brought the added perils of dust storms, lightning, and flash floods.

First light showed the road between him and the canyon clear of other travelers. Once the rain stopped, Trace began watching for tracks. At the mouth of the ravine, he found some. The mud was freshly churned by wagon wheels. The morning stage out of Prospect was ahead of Trace, possibly between him and Evelyn. He let out a heavy sigh. The wagon and its team would have obliterated any trace of a single rider.

The rain brought out all the colors of the sandstone so that the rock walls looked like sunrise preserved in stone. But it also turned the powdered dirt to a fine slick-as-snot mud that made his horse skate through the canyon and made Trace further regret not choosing a more direct route. Frothy puddles formed at the scene of the stage crash where the wreckage had been removed.

As the buckskin sloshed through, Trace ruminated on his promise to Holly. He owed her whatever peace justice could provide, hoped his service might likewise bring closure to their relationship. She was the type of woman whose affections never faltered. He'd kept her waiting for years, had rewarded her loyalty with disappointment, yet still she wished him well. Seeing her transformation, he could no longer recall his objection to her as a sheriff's wife with the same conviction he'd felt two years ago. She was respected and admired by all the town. Maybe he ought to tell Evelyn of her history. Surely the lady outlaw could achieve the same success. With that notion, Tyler's comment came unbidden to his mind. *Maybe Holly wasn't the one after all.*

When he finally neared Badger Hill, Trace saw the stage stopped at its base. He kept his left hand on the reins and raised his right, approaching slowly so as not to alarm the guard.

"Who goes there?" The man clutched the shotgun, hard eyes trained on Trace.

"Sheriff Malloy." Trace nudged his coat open to reveal his badge. "What's the trouble?"

The driver explained that they had to wait for the mud to dry up before the team could pull the coach up the incline. He asked Trace to bring word to the station regarding the delay.

"Have you seen another rider on the road?" The guard answered that he was the first traveler they'd encountered. Trace thanked them and continued to the summit.

From the top, the road wound like two snakes, north toward Prospect and south toward Tucson. He could pick out the railroad to the east and a single blocky structure that was the station. He saw a jackrabbit darting between clumps of sagebrush but no sign of Evelyn.

The trail from hill to station had been cleansed of tracks. Reaching the adobe building, Trace put the buckskin in the corral to rest and went inside. The air was stuffy from the heat of a stove, filled with the aroma of fresh-baked bread, charred bacon, and coffee. The couple that lived at and tended the stop offered Trace some of the breakfast they had ready for the stage's passengers.

He washed down a couple greasy biscuits with Arbuckle's, informed them of the delay, and asked if another traveler had come through, possibly seeking shelter from the storm. The man said that they left the stable open to such folk. His wife said she thought she'd seen a single rider head in during the storm but couldn't say how long the stranger stayed or when he left. Trace thanked them and went out to check the stable for clues.

In one stall, the hay was wet and smooshed. Trace crouched down and eyed the spot, wishing he had more experience tracking. He could imagine Evelyn huddled against the elements, soaked and shivering as she had the night of the flood. He put his hand on the rail dividing two stalls to help himself up. Noting the rough wood, he looked the boards up and down and noticed a few strands of hair snagged on a splinter. He gathered them carefully, figured them long enough to be hers.

Out in the morning sun, he held his find up to the light. The strands shone red when touched by the rays. He took the clue as confirmation, shook the hairs from his fingers, and headed south with renewed confidence.

***

Throughout the long ride, Trace remained optimistic about his chances of discovering Evelyn. After all, he'd discerned his fugitive's heading, narrowing his search from the whole of the territory to one town. But as he gazed upon the adobe maze that was Tucson, his assuredness faltered. The A. and H. Pueblo was the largest settlement in Arizona. He was looking for a flea on a buffalo's back.

Knowing that locating the sorrel would be the surest way to confirm Miss Deveraux had arrived and was still in town, Trace went straight to the nearest livery. He scanned the array of mounts, some in stalls and others in pens, but saw none the exact shade of chestnut. The owner assured him he would remember a woman traveling alone. Trace paid the man to tend to his horse and set out afoot. He inquired at the obvious places—hotels, general stores, even a bathhouse—as he came across them, covering a few blocks before reaching a telegram office.

While the operator sent his message to Prospect and leafed through unclaimed telegrams for word from Casey, Trace watched stars multiply in the darkening sky. Weariness reminded him he'd set out before dawn. The daytime businesses were closing. Trace headed for his last stop.

Lively music and the warm glow of oil lamps beckoned like a siren song. A throng of men answered the call, filing through the swinging doors into The Wishing Well. Flanking the saloon were an inn and parlor house, all sharing the same wooden architecture. The three-in-one business offered patrons whisky, women, and a place to lie their heads.

Standing outside the establishment, Trace wasn't sure whether he'd be welcomed or turned away. Stepping through the doors was like stepping back in time. His gaze went straight to the top of the stairs, to the spot he'd first laid eyes on Holly Watson. As nostalgia struck, the sense of longing was staggering. He felt it was only yesterday that he was a young cowhand with first month's pay heavy in his pocketbook, heart light with all the future's possibilities. Each time he returned, he'd sought her out, starting at that very spot. She had other men vying for her affections, some as eager to claim the hole in Holly's heart—made each time he left her—as the vacancy in her bed. But she remained his to claim, until the day he told her he would no longer return. He hadn't been back since he collected his sister two years ago, since he'd set his sights on becoming sheriff. It was an easy decision, to adjust his priorities to his new profession, but harder to live with than anticipated. She was in Prospect now. She belonged to Jerrod Kelly now. Yet Trace's eyes strayed to that spot. He felt a bittersweet echo, part past joy, part what might have been.

Familiarity was disorientating. As men shuffled in behind him, he realized he was blocking the entrance. He made his way to the bar.

"Trace Malloy." He was greeted by Louanne Fitzgerald, owner of The Wishing Well. She moved toward him, picking up a bottle and glass, and poured as she walked so that his drink was ready before she reached him. "On the house," she said, placing the whisky in front of him.

"Long time, Lou," said Trace, careful to keep his voice and emotions separate. With the same auburn hair threaded with silver that Evelyn might have in twenty years and the posture of a queen, she'd still be a handsome woman if not for the scars that marred her face. The prostitute turned businesswoman had sheltered Aimee and suffered terrible consequences at the hands of Silas Kelly.

"Yes," she agreed, her voice as dispassionate as his. Did she know he went to her competitors when in town? Did she blame him for abandoning Holly?

"I'm looking for a woman, a redhead," he said.

"Any shade in particular?" It wasn't what he meant and the sparkle in her eyes told him she knew it. "Her name is Evelyn Deveraux. She's fallen in with Wyatt Hennessy's outfit."

"None of his men are allowed in my place," said Lou. "Hennessy respects that."

"And the woman?" Lou shrugged. Trace weighed his need to find Evelyn against the possibility of causing the madame more pain. "They robbed the stage. Holly's husband was riding shotgun, was hurt." He caught the conflict in her eyes. "I promised her justice."

"Careful," said Lou. "On the flip side of that coin is revenge." Trace knew she was thinking of his mentor, Del Cooper.

"I know you have a soft spot for wayward souls," said Trace.

She met his scowl with a sad smile. "Josiah's gone. Holly's settled. You're the one I worry for now, Sheriff Malloy." She started to turn back toward waiting customers.

"Lou?" He wanted to say that he was sorry for her sorrows. Instead, he asked, "How many shades you got?"

***

The din of a piano competing with a crowd of voices rose through the floorboards, reaching Evelyn beneath the covers. After sleeping on musty straw the night before, the feather mattress was a welcome luxury. The commotion below told her the evening's business was underway. She reckoned the room—or rather the bed—would soon be needed.

Evelyn had arrived at The Wishing Well late that morning. She put her horse in the stable behind the inn, taking the time to care for the animal as she'd watched Malloy do. In the alley between inn and saloon, she found a side door propped open.

The main floor was empty except for a woman standing behind the bar, entering figures into a ledger. She had the air of a madame—at once shrewd and magnanimous. She took in Evelyn's appearance in one glance before returning to her calculations. "Are you looking for work?"

Evelyn dared not deny it, lest she be immediately turned away. "I was referred here by a friend, Grace." They'd met at The Treasure Room when Evelyn first came to Prospect. Grace had been turned away shortly thereafter but told her young friend of The Wishing Well in Tucson should she find herself in a similar situation. Too embarrassed to admit defeat, she'd gone to The Old Mare instead.

"Grace has moved on." Evelyn's shoulders slumped. She supposed even at The Wishing Well, a woman's security lasted only so long as her beauty. She looked up to find the older woman regarding her curiously. "Her name is Ralston now. She worked for me as a maid until her husband moved them to Bisbee a year ago. She told me that you might come one day."

"She did?" Evelyn wasn't sure which fact amazed her most, that Grace had found happiness or that she'd remembered her.

The woman, who introduced herself as Lou, offered Evelyn accommodations in which to clean up and sleep. After a hot bath and a quick meal, she was shown to a room in the parlor house. Alone and exhausted, she stripped to her undergarments, slipped between the sheets, and fell deep into sleep.

Tapping at the door prompted her to finally sit up. She drew a blanket up around her torso and called over her shoulder for the knocker to enter. Lou closed the door behind her, crossed arms over her chest, and studied Evelyn anew. "There's a man downstairs with an unusual request," she said. As she listened to the explanation, Evelyn could imagine him to be no other than Trace Malloy. "What do you make of it?"

"He's in love with a woman he can't have," Evelyn answered, bitterness seeping into her voice. "He wants to pretend it's her." She found herself envious of the girl Lou would choose to fulfill the role.

"I'd turn him away except he's friend to a young lady who's as dear to me as a daughter."

Evelyn's gaze dropped to her lap. "What's her name?"

"I think you know it," said Lou. "I reckon you also know the real reason he's here. Can you convince me to not turn you over?"

"My part was to shoot the lead horse and I missed," said Evelyn. "It's my fault Mr. Kelly was injured." She hung her head as Lou considered her confession.

"Do you really want to come back to this life?"

"I don't know what I want," Evelyn said, "only what I don't."

"Which is?"

"To stand in a man's shadow and feel myself diminish."

Lou nodded. "If man and woman stand side-by-side, each still casts their own shadow." She paused. "If you're willing to participate, I have a plan that might help you to some enlightenment," she said. "Come with me."

12

Trace decided that when Lou returned, he would tell her to forget it. She'd heard his unorthodox request with no reaction other than a quirk of her brow, but her absence gave him pause to reconsider his words. Without context, his solicitation came across as salacious in the most degenerative sense. It was unbecoming of any decent man and doubly so for one in service to the law. Indulging in such a selfish diversion came dangerously close to dereliction of duty. What would Del Cooper say?

Defensively, Trace reasoned that with lust purged, he could get a good night's sleep free of troublesome fantasies and start his search fresh in the morning, with priorities in order and male weakness vanquished. He tapped his empty shot glass against the bar as another worry niggled his mind. What if he got his wish and it wasn't enough to banish his desire for the red-headed vixen? He already regretted one woman. Could he stand to lament another?

A presence entered his peripheral vision. Lou spoke before he could recant his request. "I won't make my girl veil her face," she said. Trace let out the breath he'd been holding. "You'll have to take her like a stallion covers a mare." All the blood in Trace's head rushed south. His open mouth went dry as he gulped tobacco-laced air. He found himself nodding his agreement. She told him which room and turned back to her business.

Trace climbed the stairs that led to the parlor house rooms, nerves buzzing with anticipation. It really had been too long. He marveled at the tremor in his hand as he reached for the doorknob. Was it coincidence or some kind of punishment that Lou had directed him to Holly's old room? He entered and closed the door behind him. Bracing himself for disappointment, he raised his gaze from his boots. Breath gusted from his lungs.

The woman Lou had selected for him sat on her heels at the end of the bed, facing away from the door. She wore not a stitch. Her hair—exact in length and color—had been parted and pulled over each shoulder. With her chin tipped down, it veiled her face and brushed her thighs. Droplets of water glistened on her recently wetted skin. For the longest of moments, he could only stare, shocked by how perfectly she resembled his fantasy.

When he made the request, he'd reckoned he could convince his body this was the woman he craved. He wasn't prepared for the fact that he couldn't believe his eyes, that he might be so wholly duped. His nostrils flared with each breath he took. Inside his trousers, his cock swelled inch by agonizing inch.

He finally noticed the basin of water left on the mattress. He moved to the bed, seized the floating washrag and made a fist, wringing it over the base of her neck. She shuddered as rivulets coursed down her long body, flowing along her curves, pooling around her bare feet before soaking into the sheets. Goosebumps erupted over her flesh. Trace was suddenly thirsty, filled with a need too painful to be denied.

***

Evelyn heard a splash as he returned rag to basin. Through her veil of hair, she saw him place his hat over a bedpost. His knee dipped into the mattress on her right side. She imagined him gazing down the length of her spine, peering over her shoulder to glimpse the swell of her breasts. She detected a hint of whisky—he'd had one drink, maybe two. His clothes smelled of rain and fresh air. He skimmed the backs of his fingers along the top of her shoulder. When his mouth replaced them, she turned her head to the left and bit her lip.

As soon as she'd realized the intention behind his request, she'd wanted to be the woman to fulfill it. The trial she'd accepted had nothing to do with deciding whether to return to work as a lady of the line. Evelyn had no idea of resuming that life. Rather, she wanted just once to experience what it felt like to be loved. If Trace could suspend disbelief, pretend she was Holly, then Evelyn could too. She raised her right hand, gingerly touching his hair. As he sipped beads of water from her skin, her fingers curled deeper, digging into his scalp. When his teeth grazed her shoulder, Evelyn began to shiver.

"I know this is odd," said Trace, his voice gruff.

"You don't have to explain yourself to me," she said, afraid he might call off the arrangement. Dutifully, she bent forward onto her hands and knees. Bracelets around her wrists jangled as she adjusted her stance.

***

She even sounded right. It made Trace question his sanity. He hesitated further, noticing the bruises on her back. She trembled. Cold or nerves, he wondered. Seeking to soothe her, he placed a hand on her back, aligning his thumb with her spine. He massaged her waist with the pads of his fingers.

"Careful cowboy," she said in a breathy whisper. "You'll put me to sleep."

There was just enough cheekiness in her words to banish his reservations. He reached for the basin, lifted it a foot above her, and poured. She squeaked as the stream splattered her backside, spray fanning in all directions. Before she could tilt and let the water run off, he captured her waist between his hands, dipped his head and drank from the puddle at the small of her back.

He stood, water dripping down his chin, and undressed, amused by the way she curled and straightened her toes, one foot then the other, as she awaited his next move. He wanted to play with her all night. He knew he wouldn't last.

***

Evelyn heard a clunk as each boot hit the floor, the jangle of his belt loosening, then only the rustle of clothing being removed. He seemed to take his time as she quivered in anticipation. Finally, behind her, the mattress dipped under his full weight. She obligingly, eagerly, shifted her knees wider, making room for him behind her.

"Cold?" He leaned over her, blanketing her body with his. The heat of his hips and thighs eased the chill from her derriere as his chest and stomach warmed her back. Even his arms lining hers transferred heat. By the time one large palm skimmed up her belly and cupped her breast, she no longer felt cold. His cock hung, barely touching the tender folds between her thighs, full and hot enough to make her melt.

He shifted from one hand to the other, alternately stroking her with each, while his mouth left kisses up and down her back, along her sides, across her shoulders. His tongue returned to a spot along her spine. When she sighed, he pinched her nipple and warned, "Don't fall asleep."

In retaliation, she shifted balance to one forearm, reached back and seized his cock, sliding her fist down his length. She was rewarded by a blast of hot air delivering expletives against her skin. She hoped he didn't ruin it, prayed he'd spare her the mortification of hearing him call out the other woman's name.

***

Trace growled as her grip made his balls tighten. He reared up, swatted her buttocks, and she released him. She arched her back as if inviting him to spank the other cheek. Instead, he hefted his cock, spreading the dew she'd wrung from him down his shaft. He slid the head over her anus, down to dip into her folds. She moaned and slid her knees apart, opening for him. Then she sank to her elbows, the new angle inviting him to culminate the fantasy. She was perfect, thought Trace again and again, over and over, claiming her like he couldn't claim another.

The clink of glasses accompanied the crescendo of piano climbing from the cacophony of voices in the saloon below. Footfalls sounded in the hall as another of Lou's ladies escorted her customer to one of the other rooms. Spent and satisfied in equal measure, Trace willed himself to rise. The noise reminded him where he was, who he was and wasn't with. The woman lay panting into the mattress, wild auburn hair wantonly splayed over bed and body. He found her fingers entwined with his but couldn't remember when he'd taken her hand. He tried to recall whether he'd actually chanted Evelyn's name or if it had only reverberated through his mind. He wanted to roll her over and kiss her lips, but they wouldn't be the same lips he'd kissed through jailhouse bars. So, he contented himself with pressing his mouth to the small scar he'd discovered adjacent to her spine.

Trace dressed, unsteady after the exertion. He emptied the contents of his billfold into the empty basin, taking back enough for a few drinks and a room for the night. Though more than her rate, it still wasn't enough in his estimation. She'd been perfect.

***

When the door closed behind him again, Evelyn rolled to her side. She didn't know when she'd started to cry, if the tears were joy or sorrow. All she knew was that Trace Malloy had gone and taken her heart with him.

***

Trace decided that the lightness of his pocketbook was a small price to pay for the serenity he felt as he reentered the saloon. Lou met him at the bar with another whisky. When he asked if there were any vacancies at the inn, she produced the room key she'd reserved for him. He paid her then raised his glass, making a silent toast to the whore who'd broken the spell Evelyn Deveraux had over him.

He left by the side door, crossing the alley that made a buffer between boisterous watering hole and restful inn. Trace found his room, stripped to his union suit, and with pent-up lust finally exorcised from his loins, fell into sleep.

When he awoke the next morning, the whisky had worn off, leaving him with a mild headache and slight chill. He shifted onto his side and a pang of longing struck him as he viewed the empty expanse of mattress beside him. He found himself wishing she were there, wishing he could draw her back against his chest and breathe deeply through auburn hair. The feeling was too close to one he'd experienced before.

He dressed and left through the inn's side door. Glancing sidelong, he noted the stable and decided it prudent to check for the sorrel. The stalls accommodated a few horses belonging to guests still asleep in the inn. Evelyn's mount wasn't among them.

Inside the saloon, Lou was stationed behind the bar, cleaning glasses. "Checking out?"

"The woman from last night," said Trace. "I need to see her."

"She must have done you good." Lou smiled. "But the parlor house is closed."

Trace said, "I wanted to ask her about the bruises." In truth, he needed to view her in the light and sobriety of day, to see that she was an ordinary woman, to know he wouldn't require fantasy incarnate to banish the feeling with which he'd awoken.

"You know I don't stand for any mistreatment of my girls."

"Of course not," said Trace. "But—"

"This isn't your jurisdiction, sheriff."

"Will you allow me to talk to her?"

"She's gone."

Trace returned to the telegraph office only to find his deputy hadn't replied to last night's telegram. He sent another and awaited its receipt on a bench out front. He chewed his cuticles and tried to reason away the ache in his chest. Evelyn Deveraux was a woman in trouble, whether she knew it or not. It was only natural for him to want to help her, to wish to gain her trust. It was his sworn duty—to protect. He forgave himself his attraction.

She'd been trained to seduce men, had tempted him since he arrested her, and he'd been at a disadvantage, having gone too long without a woman. That was rectified. What worried him was the knowing look in Lou's eyes.

The telegraph officer interrupted his solitude, saving Trace from his ruminations. The message from Prospect read: *Nothing to report. No sign of Hennessy.*

He prowled the boardwalk, thinking back to their conversations at the farmhouse. He wondered where he'd gone wrong, why she'd fled. He noted there were already a hundred bodies starting their day on this one street. And Tucson had scores more. Whatever small, nameless settlement Deveraux came from had likely been swallowed by the larger town. It might take weeks of inquiry for him to find anyone who knew of her relations. He tried to guess how many liveries there were, how many private stables. He recalled Tyler asking her about Promise and her reply that she didn't know it. Trace's stride faltered. What if she'd lied?

Up until that point, he'd believed her a victim—of desperation, of misplaced loyalty, of misguided affection. What if she was complicit in the gang's operation, not just Hennessy's bedwarmer? He'd have to assume every interaction, starting with her arrest at The Old Mare, had been by design. If she'd been sent to handle him, she'd succeeded better than she knew. The woman had his sympathy, his chivalry, his very heart, all on one stick. He realized that if the gang had a hideout in the ghost town, the clue at the stage stop might have been planted to lead him astray. Evelyn might never have come to Tucson. Trace sighed, feeling a fool. Then he headed to collect his horse.

13

Evelyn left Tucson at first light, right after purchasing a new hat to rid herself of the night's earnings. She couldn't chance running into Malloy with foolish heart on her sleeve when he only had eyes for another, when he only wanted her to get at her boss. She craved distance, as many miles between them as her horse would endure. Thankfully, the sorrel was well-rested.

She rode for Promise, the only destination she could think of to go. Wyatt hadn't entrusted her with his plans or the gang's future whereabouts. Maybe he expected her to forego loyalty if caught, as is the way with thieves. She hoped she was stronger than that. She at least had the satisfaction of having fulfilled her mission. Malloy might scour the Old Pueblo for days. With any luck, the job would be done before the sheriff crossed the county line back into his own bailiwick. Evelyn pretended none of her relief was for Malloy's sake.

The wind dried her tears as her thoughts circled round the events that had led to her, a willing and wanton sacrifice, bucking beneath Malloy. A kiss seduced through jailhouse bars. A rescue amidst a storm. An introduction to his family. A proposition that left her wishing for more. When had there been time to fall in love?

The sight of the stage stop surprised her. She felt she'd barely left Tucson, yet the sorrel had transported her twenty miles. She bypassed the adobe building, Badger Hill, the canyon, and especially the farmhouse, reaching Promise as the sun dipped toward the western horizon.

She was hitching her horse outside the old jail when one of the Bradford brothers appeared in the doorway. "What are you doing here?" she asked.

"Hennessy ordered us to stay behind and watch out for you."

"Us?" A warning whistle sounded from the lookout position across the street. Another Bradford brother signaled that they had company.

***

Trace entered Promise with reins in one hand and gun in the other, eyes darting between windows and rooftops, ready to escape through the nearest alley at first sign of an ambush. He'd surveyed the ghost town from a distance and skirted both sides, glimpsing only the sorrel hitched about mid-stretch.

Next, he ventured down the main drag, shrugging off the tingle that crawled up his spine as he passed the shot-up fronts of the old inn and building opposite. He came across the days-old remains of a bonfire, ashes scattered by recent rains. Moving from one end of town to the other, he stayed in the saddle, knowing he could make a quicker getaway if already mounted. But for the swish of the sorrel's tail and his own presence, the place was still and silent as a graveyard.

He doubled back, figuring that if any bandits were holed up in the abandoned structures, he'd have already drawn their attention. He dismounted and secured the buckskin ten feet down from the chestnut mare, out of line-of-sight of anyone who might chance to glance out the doorway. He stayed on the street, dust dampening his footfalls, moving with measured stride so as not to spook the other horse.

He stood close to the animal, using it to conceal his presence. The Winchester remained in its scabbard. As he stroked the horse's neck, he spied Evelyn inside the building which the cage behind her gave away as the old Promise jailhouse. Trace wondered what she was doing there, for whom she waited.

He holstered his Colt, keeping his hand on the pistol grip as he gave one last glance up and down the street and boardwalks. A light breeze made the dust and ash drift over the ground like mist. Evelyn turned toward the doorway as Trace stepped up onto the sidewalk. Green eyes failed to register surprise. Could she have been waiting for him? Had she changed her mind about aiding him after discovering Hennessy gone?

He stepped through the door and froze at the sound of guns being cocked. He was flanked by two men, each with a pistol pointed at the side of his head. He wondered about the likelihood of them shooting one another if he moved. Chances were slim he'd remain unscathed. Before he could decide on a course of action, the man on the right stepped forward and plucked Trace's revolver from its holster.

"Keep walking, Malloy," the other man ordered.

Trace stepped into the cell. Evelyn shut the door. It locked with a resounding clank.

***

Deciding they deserved a celebratory drink, the Bradford brothers led the way across the street, congratulating one another on their catch. Silently, Evelyn followed. She'd managed to school her expression during the standoff, hiding her emotions from three men. But when she stepped off the boardwalk, her limbs wobbled like jelly and butterflies bubbled up from her belly. By the time Evelyn joined them, the brothers had uncorked a bottle of whisky and were passing it back and forth.

"What are we going to do with him?" said Ben. "Bring him to Hennessy? Lynch him?"

"Leave him to rot," replied Beau. "We'll be rich and gone."

Evelyn stood behind the old cashier's counter, using it for balance as she reclaimed her nerves. She listened as the brothers' voices began to slur.

Ben said, "What if someone happens by and sets him loose?"

"Who's going to wander through this wreck?" Ben shrugged but Beau reconsidered. "So, we kill him before we leave."

"Do I get a drink?" Their heads turned in sync as though they'd forgotten her. Evelyn crossed her arms and leaned her elbows on the counter. Two sets of eyes drifted to her chest. In answer, Beau wagged the bottle at her, inviting her to come take it. She straightened, turned her back, put her hands on the surface behind her, and with a hop was seated atop it. She tucked her legs and spun about, dropping down on the other side.

When she reached for the whisky, Beau raised it over his head, forcing her to stretch for it. "How long you boys been waiting here?" She took a long pull, tipping her head back, aware that their eyes were fixed upon her throat. She handed the bottle back to Beau, feigned steadying herself against his arm. She felt the flush strong liquor brought to her flesh, unknotted her bandana and used it to fan her face.

A flutter of lashes was all the encouragement Beau required to slip an arm around her hips. "Go check the prisoner," he ordered his brother.

"He ain't going nowhere," said Ben. As his brother began to pick at the buttons of her shirt, Evelyn felt another pair of hands grip her ass. They fell away when Beau glared at him over her shoulder. Ben shuffled toward the door. "When you're done, I want my turn."

When she lifted her chin to take another drink, Beau nosed down her shirt, slobbering into her cleavage. She took ahold of his collar and tugged him back. "Your clothes stink."

"I'll take them off," he offered with a gap-toothed grin.

"While you do that, I've got to use the privy." She forced a smile and went out the back door, taking the whisky with her. She took a swig, swished and spat, then jogged around the corner, through an alley, back to Main Street.

***

Trace had found himself on the wrong side of a cell door a few times in his life but not once since he'd decided to pursue the office of sheriff. He never expected to be put there by the criminals he sought to lock up. The key hung on a nail on the wall across from the door. Trace reckoned he should feel glad it hadn't been lost. He'd tested each board in the walls and floor, finding the old jail as sound as the day it was built. He heard footsteps and turned to face the younger of the two men.

"Short straw get you guard duty?"

"Just giving my brother and the lady some privacy." He didn't look happy about it and neither was Trace. The implications put a sour taste in his mouth. "I get her next," the man bragged, oblivious to the dangerous look shot at him.

"You're one of the Bradford brothers, ain't you?"

"Benjamin Bradford." The young man puffed out his chest.

"My brother and I used to drive cattle through Texas."

"We ever get any of your herd?"

"Not ours." He watched Ben pull his Colt from his belt and begin inspecting the confiscated gun. "What brought you to Arizona?" Trace heard three of the brothers had been killed by cowboys protecting their cattle. "Not much for change of scenery."

Ben snorted his agreement. "More lucrative though."

"Even after Easton Stine takes his cut?"

The other man stopped fondling the gun and smirked at Trace. "On the wrong side of those bars for interrogating, ain't you, sheriff?" He walked over to an old desk and busied himself with rooting through the drawers, apparently finding little of interest by the speed with which he shut one and moved to the next.

Evelyn appeared in the doorway, the sound of her footsteps covered by slamming drawers, a bottle in her hand. Her shirt gaped open at the neck, revealing a delicate collarbone and the ivory material of whatever she wore beneath. She glanced at Ben's back, at the key on the wall, then focused on Trace. She crooked her finger at him, took a swig of liquor, and crossed the room, swaying slightly. Trace met her at the bars with a suspicious scowl. He didn't quite buy her hooded eyes and sleepy smile but didn't stop her reaching into the cell and draping one arm over his shoulder. Her eyes fixed on his mouth and as she scraped her teeth over her bottom lip, he saw that it was bruised.

She let the bottle slip through her fingers—it glanced off her boot, thudded and rolled—and reached for him, taking hold of his shirt and hauling them toward one another, against the bars. Beyond her, Trace saw Ben turn.

She kissed him and he tasted whisky. There couldn't be enough to intoxicate, yet his head spun. Hating that she could handle him with such ease, he retaliated the only way he could, giving her bruised lip a hard suck. He heard Ben's voice demand, "What's the big idea?" And her mouth was ripped from his as she was spun around.

She stumbled against the outlaw, laughing as he wrestled to steady her without unbalancing himself. No sooner were they stable than Evelyn brushed her lips against Ben's, making an offer no randy young man could refuse. He kissed her back, she leaned into him, and the pair collided with the cell door.

Trace snarled and backed away, reckoning that he'd have to watch them go at one another, right there. Bradford's arms banded her waist. He leveraged his back against the iron bars and bumped his groin against Evelyn's thighs. When she put her hands on his shoulders and arched her spine, he ground his face into her breasts. Over his head, Evelyn opened her eyes and glared at Trace. It wasn't until she spoke that he understood the call to action. "A little help here?"

Before young Bradford knew the game had changed, Trace snaked his arm through the bars and trapped the man's throat in the crook of his elbow. Evelyn disengaged herself, retreating to the desk where her confederate had left Trace's revolver. Trace held on as the man thrashed until he passed out. He lowered the unconscious jailer to the floor while Evelyn fetched the key.

"Evelyn," he prompted when she hesitated. She was shaking and her lip was bleeding.

"I'm not going back with you," she said, "not as your prisoner."

"Open the door," he urged, aware that the commotion might have alerted Ben's older brother, that he was as good as a fish in a barrel trapped within the cell.

"Not as your witness."

She had his freedom in one hand, his weapon in the other. The easiest thing was to agree. She turned the key in the lock. Hinges shrieked as he pushed the door open. He took the gun from her trembling hand and returned it to his holster.

"You should go," she said, glancing across the street. "I ought to get back." She moved to lead the way out the door.

Trace caught her arm. "Tell me why," he said.

"It was my mission to deal with you." She raised her chin. "Mine alone."

"Is that the real reason?"

"What other could I have?"

For once, he hoped she lied. He didn't know where she'd gone after the farmhouse, what had happened to her while he was in Tucson, but he sensed something altered in her as well. Something or someone had shaken her confidence, put a chink in her resolve. He wanted to shake the truth from her before she recovered either. There was no time.

"What in tarnation?" The exclamation came from across the street. Beau Bradford stood framed by the doorway, wearing only baggy and faded underwear and boots. The pistol must have been in his hand, but Trace didn't see it until the barrel was swinging in his direction. He shoved Evelyn aside and snatched the Colt from his hip, firing even as he aimed.

There was an explosion of gunfire from each side. Bullets must have zinged past each other. The sorrel bucked and fought its tether. Trace's second and third shots were the first to find their mark. Beau crumpled, half inside the building, half out. Black powder hung on the breeze. On her backside on the boardwalk, Evelyn fixated on the downed man's motionless brown boots.

"Evelyn, are you all right?" Trace had to ask twice.

She shook her head. "This wasn't supposed to happen." Her voice held a hollow inflection.

Inside the jail, the younger man began to stir. Trace fetched manacles from his saddle bag, confiscated Ben's gun and bound his hands. He crossed the street, gripped the fallen man under the arms, and dragged him down the wood walk, out of sight of his brother.

"Where do I find their horses?"

Evelyn showed him the storage outbuilding that was being used as a makeshift stable. He readied the animals and worried what to do with her. Whichever way her loyalties had been leaning, he reckoned the death of Beau Bradford changed everything. He wished he knew how. He found her loitering outside the jailhouse, not daring to go in and face Ben. She paled when he told her he needed her help to load the body, but she did so without a fuss.

Inside, the bound man began to holler, having discovered his predicament. "I've got my prisoner," said Trace. "I'm still hoping you'll be my witness." It had to be her choice—he'd agreed. But he didn't want to subject her to whatever blame the surviving brother might fling at her during the ride back to Prospect. He untied the sorrel from the hitching post and passed her the reins. "Don't take more than a few days to decide."

She mounted and pointed her horse toward the distant hills. Trace watched her ride away before turning back to the jail and the long evening ahead.

14

Trace arrived in Prospect as the sun was setting. The town was awash in an amber glow, but the moon and stars were already visible above, awaiting their turn to shine. Likewise, the saloons, brothels, and gambling dens were lit up, awaiting a surge of customers. Folk could work away the day, but some found the dark too lonely for sleep, were willing to trade all they earned for company in passing the night.

There were more direct routes to the jailhouse, but Trace led the two extra horses down the main drag, past The Old Mare, right under Easton Stine's nose. He pretended not to see the figure watching from the balconet.

"Sheriff." When Casey hailed him from the boardwalk, Trace waved him over.

He held up a hand to stop the excitement in his deputy's eyes from bubbling out his mouth. "Untie the last horse," Trace instructed. "Bring that man to the coroner then meet me at the jail." Once Casey had the lead to Beau's horse in hand, Trace continued to the jailhouse.

He hitched both horses then helped his prisoner dismount. Luckily, his deputy had left the oil lamp burning inside. Trace marched the other Bradford into the cell.

The boarding house would be serving supper and Trace was weary, but he reckoned his prisoner was just as tired. He hoped it would work to his advantage. To get the man talking, he asked, "Are you the youngest of your brothers?"

Ben nodded. "There were seven of us. Four when we left Texas." He paused. "Now three."

"I have one brother," said Trace. "I reckon he wasn't ready for half the adventures I led him on."

"Well, I'm ready for anything." He sounded like Casey.

"You ready to lose more brothers?"

"I'll lose them for sure if I betray them." The young man set his lips into a firm line and stuck out his chin.

Trace reckoned it was too soon to get any information out of him regarding Stine or Hennessy. He chose a different subject to loosen his prisoner's tongue. "Tell me about Deveraux," he said. "How'd she come to be part of the outfit?"

Ben shrugged. "Wyatt met her gambling at The Old Mare. She can't ride or shoot worth a darn. And she's too good to spread her legs for the likes of us." He let out a short laugh. "Who knew all it took was getting her drunk." His eyes darkened as he looked up at Trace. "This is her fault."

When Casey returned, Trace motioned him outside. "Need me to see to the horses, sheriff?"

"I'll do it," said Trace. He asked if the younger man could stay and guard the prisoner. Casey assured him that he was up to the task. "Don't ask him no questions," said Trace. "Let him talk if he wants, listen good, and I'll hear it in the morning."

***

After tending to the horses, rather than seek his bed as much as he needed it, Trace took a long walk. He left the welcoming merriment of Main Street to roam darker and quieter avenues on the edge of Prospect's red light district. Only the ruby glow of oil lamps through burgundy drapes told him he'd come to the right place. Outside, the house was an oddity, with architectural charms that seemed superfluous in a rough mining town. But inside, the illusion became complete.

A very young and exceptionally lovely woman answered his knock. "Do you have an appointment?" the hostess asked in a sweet voice, though his attire surely made it clear he couldn't have afforded one.

"I'm here on official business." Trace indicated his star. "If I could speak to the madame?"

She led him into the foyer, and with a whisper of silk dress the only sound, went to inform her mistress. Trace found himself gawking at the décor—rich colors with crystal and gilded accents—designed to make one forget he was on the frontier and not in some Old World royal court. From where he stood, Trace could glimpse into the parlor where gentlemen sipped fine liquor and smoked expensive cigars whilst awaiting even more priceless pleasures. He recognized the mayor and owner of Prospect's best hotel among the patrons.

Gliding back into the room in near silence, the hostess told Trace the madame would see him. He followed her into another parlor, personal to The Treasure Room's matron. She was older than expected. The marks of breeding almost obscured the fact that despite her jewelry and clothing, she was not beautiful. She gave him a practiced smile that didn't soften her shrewd eyes.

"I can't imagine what I can do for you," she said.

"I'm looking for information."

"Discussing my clients would be detrimental to my business—"

"About an employee," said Trace. "A former one."

Her nostrils flared as she took a long and deep breath through a narrow nose. "Very well, but I'll ask a favor in return."

Trace pursed his lips. "So long as it doesn't conflict with my oath of office."

"A man of his word?" She raised an eyebrow. "How provincial."

"The favor?" asked Trace.

"Easton Stine is trying to entice my girls to go work for him. I want him banned from my establishment. I think it would be taken more seriously coming from a fellow lawman."

"I'll relay the message," said Trace.

The madame nodded. Trace reckoned it was all the thanks she'd condescend to give. "Which girl?"

"Evelyn Deveraux," he said. She looked at the ceiling as if struggling to recall. "Tall. Long auburn hair. Green eyes."

"Sad eyes," the woman supplied.

"Yes." He'd never thought to coin that flash of pained vulnerability as such.

"A little sorrow is alluring," she said. "Too much attracts the wrong element."

"The wrong—"

"Sadists." Trace immediately thought of Silas Kelly. She continued, "Evelyn Deveraux isn't her real name, of course." She chuckled at his obvious surprise. "Many of the girls invent new identities for themselves as a way to forget the lives from whence they came."

"Why did she leave your employment?"

"I run a business," she said. "Like the grocer, I must keep the selection fresh. If a man wants an old favorite, he turns to his wife."

"The girl who answered the door—"

"Her first time will fetch a premium in a year, maybe two. For now, she keeps the wine flowing, warms them with a smile, and satisfies the odd exotic request." Smirking at Trace's blank expression, she explained, "It's more popular amongst the French." She laughed when he grimaced. "Don't knock it until you've tried it, cowboy. Will that be all?"

"Do you know," said Trace, "does Miss Deveraux have people in these parts? Anyplace she might go if in trouble?"

"My bet would be Stine," she said. "He likes the sorrow." She reminded him of their bargain and showed him out.

Trace stood outside, momentarily disorientated back out in the desert night with dirt under his boots and the smell of creosote and manure on the breeze. When he looked up, he decided the stars glittered far prettier than any crystal in the house of sin.

Again, he wandered the lonely streets, trying to banish the idea of Evelyn on her knees looking up at him with those eyes, worrying that deep down, Easton Stine, Silas Kelly, and himself all had something in common.

***

Trace fell into bed, head pounding with contrary emotions and insides twisted up over what he was powerless to control. Mercifully, sleep pulled him under, and he awoke with all in perspective. He had a job to do, an oath to uphold. Duty would lead to resolution in time. He imagined Evelyn awakening with similar clarity. He'd treated her fairly, never taking advantage. Despite her flirtations, his fantasies were known only to him and would remain so. He'd offered her help, had to trust that when she was ready, she'd seek him out. He told himself it would be soon, maybe today. And when this was over, only when it was over, he could decide whether to act on his feelings for her.

He was one of the first to breakfast. He found the morning paper already featured news of Beau Bradford's death and Ben's arrest in connection with the stage robbery, probably confirmed by Casey and the coroner. The reporter would undoubtedly be by that day for Trace's statement.

Arriving at the jail, Trace found deputy and prisoner still dozing on their respective cots. Casey informed him that Ben had gone to sleep shortly after Trace left. Trace dismissed him to get some rest and spent the morning catching up on paperwork.

Ben awoke and ate the meal Trace brought with from the boarding house. "My brothers will want to give Beau a proper burial," he said. Trace told him the news was in the paper. Ben nodded. "Someone will read it and let them know." He seemed reluctant to talk, so Trace allowed him to sit in silence. If Evelyn showed, he wouldn't need to interrogate Bradford.

Trace paced the jail for exercise, stood out on the boardwalk for fresh air and a change of scenery. Really, he watched for her. It was past noon when Casey returned.

"I came by way of The Old Mare," he said. Trace asked if there'd been any sign of Hennessy or the remaining Bradford brothers. "No, but Deveraux's horse was hitched out front."

"At The Mare?" Casey nodded. "You're certain it was hers, the sorrel with the star on its forehead." Casey nodded again. Trace stared down the street in the direction of the saloon until his deputy cleared his throat and asked a second time if Trace wanted him to investigate what she might be doing there. "No," said Trace. "I'll go."

He felt his anxieties of the previous night swimming in the back of his mind as he walked. He told himself that she might not have gone to the saloon to reunite with Hennessy or find sanctuary with Stine, but the fact that stuck in his craw, that he couldn't deny, was that she hadn't come to him. Perhaps she hadn't wanted to face young Bradford.

Inside, the saloon was empty but for a few regulars whittling away the day. Evelyn was nowhere to be seen. Trace rested his elbows on the counter and waited for the old bar dog to approach.

"She gave me her rifle." He reached for something low on a shelf, raising the Winchester for Trace to glimpse. "No laws broken today."

"She upstairs?" asked Trace. To his relief, the bartender said that she'd left but told him she'd be back. "Say where she was going?"

"I mind my own," the man said, "but you're welcome to wait."

15

Evelyn finally knocked at the door she'd been standing outside for the past ten minutes. A woman's voice called out, "Please come in." She hesitated and heard, "It's unlocked." Evelyn entered and discovered the small brunette struggling to remove a kettle from where it hung over the fire. Holly turned and froze, smile faltering. "I thought you were someone else." She poured the steaming water from heavy kettle into a waiting teapot.

"The sheriff?" asked Evelyn.

Mrs. Kelly returned the vessel to its hanger and faced her unexpected guest. "The doctor," she said. Evelyn chewed the inside of her cheek while Holly placed a cover over the pot to insulate it while the tea infused. To Evelyn's surprise, she invited her to sit. "It'll be ready in a few minutes."

"Got anything stronger?" Holly poured brandy into two hand-painted teacups. Evelyn couldn't suppress a nervous laugh. "It's been years since I drank from a cup with flowers on it."

Sitting opposite, they studied one another's clothing, avoiding eye contact. "Do you know," said Holly, "that you and I have similar histories?" Evelyn nodded. She'd guessed as much from Louanne Fitzgerald's claim of friendship. Holly said, "I reckon we had similar hopes too."

"Vain hopes," said Evelyn. "At least for me."

"Is that why you dress as you do? You'd rather forsake convention than risk disappointment?"

Evelyn shrugged. "At least I won't find myself lying with one man and bringing pie to another."

Holly straightened. "Independence isn't freedom from heartache," she said. "Neither does having loved and lost diminish the promise of a second chance. I don't believe the heart loses its capacity to love."

Maybe that was the difference between them, thought Evelyn. At her core, Holly possessed a self-replenishing well of optimism, while Evelyn's marrow, poisoned by reality, grew increasingly bitter. She thought she'd been close to satisfaction, until Malloy opened old wounds and awakened dormant dreams.

She'd spent the night at the cave where they had sheltered from the storm, trying to reconcile her feelings for him with her mission. She'd devised a strategy that might spare her heart and his life. If it worked, she would never have to see him again. Holly was the key.

As if on cue, the other woman said, "I hope Trace won't deny himself his second chance."

"He won't get one, if he keeps after Hennessy," said Evelyn. "There's men that want him dead." She felt a twinge of guilt as worry flooded cornflower eyes but reckoned those tears would save Malloy's life. "He'll listen to you—"

"Holly?" There was a shuffle in the hall. Evelyn turned to see Jerrod Kelly propped up with a crutch, chest bare and bruised, ribs wrapped. His wife jumped up and went to him.

Evelyn did her best not to eavesdrop on their whispers, though the tenderness in their hushed tones made her eyes misty and her throat burn. She told herself it was the brandy. But she was thinking about what it said about a man that he would take the woman broken by another and seek to restore her, to make her whole again. He couldn't expect Holly to love him with the same hope, the same innocence with which she'd loved Trace Malloy, yet he didn't regard her any less worthy for it. This was Silas Kelly's brother, Evelyn thought once again. But if Silas had been capable of such devotion, something had killed it long before Evelyn met him.

Holly persuaded her husband to go back to bed. Returning to the parlor area, she gave Evelyn a considering look. "Though we have much in common, I can't imagine being in your… boots."

Evelyn stood as another knock sounded. She followed Holly to the door. When it opened, the doctor greeted them with a nod as he passed between them on his way down the hall.

Holly said, "I hope you won't deny yourself a second chance either, Miss Deveraux." Evelyn stepped over the threshold as Mrs. Kelly moved to close the door. It shut with her outside, wondering if Holly had just agreed or refused to help.

She made her way back to The Old Mare, along a street parallel to Main where she wouldn't pass within sight of the jailhouse. She didn't notice the man watching her approach from the livery, until he crossed and followed her into an alley. She heard him move to overtake her and whirled.

"You shouldn't be here," said Wyatt.

"I didn't know where else to go." She reminded him that he'd given her no way to contact him but through Stine.

"I left two men in Promise. Now one's dead and the other's taken prisoner. What the hell happened?"

"Ben and Beau were drunk," said Evelyn. "Malloy got the better of them." She neglected to disclose her role in his escape. "In truth, it was your mistake too."

"How's that?"

"They shouldn't have been there. You gave the job of dealing with Malloy to me."

Wyatt massaged his chin with one hand as he eyed her. "Stine called a meeting. If he backs out, we lose our advantage."

Evelyn found herself hoping the deal was off. "There will be other opportunities," she said.

"None like this. Some renegades never see a score like we stand to make. A man could get by the rest of his days if he's clever."

It was her turn to scrutinize. "You're quitting the gang." When he didn't deny it, she said, "What happened to making our own luck?"

"In this business, you fold while you're ahead," said Wyatt.

"What am I to do?"

"You'll have money enough to do whatever you wish. Come on," he said. "Let's see if we can convince Stine to ante up."

***

Trace had been at the saloon a half hour when the door to the second-floor office opened and Easton Stine stepped out. He checked his pocket watch with a scowl as if he too waited for someone. Then he gripped the banister and surveyed the floor below, scowl deepening as he caught sight of Trace.

The batwing doors flapped inward and Wyatt Hennessy entered with Evelyn directly behind. He strode toward the stairs and she followed, though her pace slowed a step when Trace rose from his stool. He met her at the bottom landing as Wyatt started up. He gestured for her to stop, but she shook her head and followed her boss. He hesitated only a heartbeat before continuing after them. At the top, he quickened his pace and was on her heels as she crossed into Stine's office.

"This is a private meeting, sheriff," the saloon-owner said with a sneer, blocking the door, expecting Trace to leave. Instead, he shouldered past, caught Evelyn's arm, and directed her through a set of French doors into an adjoining room. As he shut them in, he heard Stine complain, "Those are my quarters."

"Let's talk." Hennessy's voice drew the businessman away.

"What are you doing?" Evelyn hissed.

"I've got a prisoner who's going to tell his boss you're a traitor," Trace bluffed, jerking his thumb back toward the other room. "So, what are *you* doing?"

"I already told him what I did," she lied. "And why."

"He bought it?" Trace scoffed.

"It's the truth." She lifted her chin and brushed by him, away from the muffled conversation going on beyond the French doors.

"Nothing you say is the truth." Trace stalked after her. "He's infatuated. Stine's infatuated." She reached the opposite wall and turned to face him. He closed the distance, shaking his head. "Have you ever met a man who's immune?"

"You tell me."

"Don't start." It struck him that they were standing in Easton Stine's bedroom. The four-poster was almost as big as Trace's accommodations at the boarding house. "You been here before?" The answer was in her shifting eyes. His lip curled.

"Always ready to believe the worst of me?" She lifted her chin. But the bravado wasn't there. Instead, he watched her attempt to blink away hurt. "Please leave," she whispered.

"I'll go," he said, "but I want something first." He put hands on her hips. Her eyes widened as he backed her up against the wall. "Tell me your name. Your real name." He was certain it was something neither of the men in the other room knew. He realized he needed it.

"Libby," she said. She gave it to him readily, without innuendo or teasing smile.

The name didn't suit the woman she'd become, but it might once have matched the girl she'd been. "Short for?"

She gave a slight, sad smile. "Just Libby."

Trace forced himself to release her when he wanted to draw her closer. "Let me help you."

"It's not your help that I want."

There came a sharp knock on the door and Hennessy called from the other side. "Time to ride, Deveraux." Evelyn stepped around him, practically dashing from the room. When Trace walked back into the office, she and the bandit leader were gone.

Stine was waiting. "I don't want you near my property." Trace didn't think he meant The Old Mare.

"That reminds me," he said. "I was asked to tell you that you've been banned from The Treasure Room."

***

Trace marched back to the jailhouse. He rapped on the bars to rouse his prisoner. "Time to make a deal," he said as Bradford blinked at him. "Tell me about Stine. I want to know what he's got going with Hennessy."

Casey rose from behind the desk. Ben glanced between him and Trace. "Stine has ways of knowing what's said about him."

Trace signaled his deputy, jerking his chin toward the door. When the bewildered man didn't budge, he barked, "Horne, take a walk." Once Casey shuffled out, Trace said, "I'll release you, pretend your brothers were never involved. All I want are Hennessy and Stine." The deputy's absence did little to relax Bradford. "Y'all can make a fresh start, stop losing brothers to make a rich man richer."

"All right," his prisoner agreed. "But Stine's never directly involved. Rather he has ways of uncomplicating a job for us."

"Was Stine the one who wanted to ambush the stage in the canyon?" Ben nodded. It seemed to confirm the town marshal's motive to make Trace look incompetent in the coming election. He asked Bradford what scheme they were hatching next. "What's Stine's role?"

"Only Hennessy knows—that's the way Stine wants it. I only know my part."

"Which is?"

A soft knock interrupted Ben's response. "Hold on," said Trace. For a moment, he dared to hope Evelyn had returned, until he opened the door and felt only disappointment. "Holly, I'm busy."

"It's important," she said.

"Is it Jerrod?" Instantly, he felt guilty for the dismissal. He stepped out onto the boardwalk, closing the door to afford them some privacy. "Has he taken a bad turn?"

"He's well. But Evelyn Deveraux came to see me."

"Just now?"

"No, earlier."

He told Holly he'd walk her home. He popped his head back into the jailhouse, telling Bradford, "I'll be back in five minutes. Try to think of any details you've missed."

When he offered Holly his arm, she clutched it. "Trace, she said that they're men meaning to kill you."

"Did she say where she was going?"

"Did you hear what I said?" asked Holly.

"Stine's crooked, but he only wants my job," said Trace.

Holly paled. "Town Marshal Stine?"

"I'm going to expose him and get justice for Jerrod."

"Don't go after him," she said. "I'm not asking for me."

They were almost to the Kelly home when the shooting started. Two gunshots sounded from the way they'd come.

"She's in love with you," said Holly, but Trace didn't hear. He turned his attention from her as three more shots were fired.

16

Trace charged down the boardwalk, slowing a few strides short of his deputy who stood in the jailhouse doorway, gun drawn. He put a hand on the younger man's shoulder. It fell away as he took in the scene.

Black powder hung in the air. The cell door was open, and Benjamin Bradford lay sprawled out on the floor, blood pooling around his body.

"He was trying to escape," said Casey.

Trace sidestepped him, coming to stand over the prisoner. "Why would he try to escape?" He noted the crimson splatter on the cell wall opposite the bars and the tendril of smoke rising from smoldering clothing. He crouched down to check the man's hands, finding them empty. "I reckon you unlocked this cell." Trace stood and fixed his deputy with a hard gaze.

Casey's mouth opened and closed before he could manage a sound. "Sheriff," he said. "I tell you he was trying—"

"Why would he try to escape? I was going to let him go."

"Let him go," parroted Casey.

"How long have you worked for Stine?" Trace started toward him.

The other man stood his ground. His eyes narrowed and his neck reddened as his befuddled expression tightened into one of petulance. "You've been telling me all along what a thankless job this is, what a lost cause honor is. You've given me one menial task after another, yet you're surprised when I jump at the opportunity for action and reward."

His words brought Trace up short. He'd tried to pass on Del Cooper's wisdom. He wondered how his teachings could be so misunderstood, how sacrifice could be mistaken for weakness and duty for foolishness. "Shooting an unarmed man is cowardice," said Trace. "Not to mention murder."

Casey scoffed. "This town is corrupt. You're the only one trying to do the right thing. No man gets ahead by following along. And for that matter, no woman is wooed by noble intentions. Not in this town."

Trace tore the badge from Casey's vest. "You don't deserve this," he said, voice husky, eyes blazing. "And you don't deserve my sister neither."

He didn't even try to deflect the blow as Casey clobbered him upside the head with the empty pistol still in hand. "Once Stine is sheriff, I'll have it back. As for marrying Aimee, you won't be around to contest it."

Pain fed rage which quashed the burn of betrayal. Trace drove his fist into his former deputy's gut. When the man doubled over, he gave him a mighty shove out the jailhouse door. They faced off on the boardwalk. Casey lunged at Trace, and the two tumbled off the edge into the street, trading blows in a cloud of dust. It took two bystanders to haul Trace off his opponent. By the time he struggled free of their restraining arms, Casey Horne had fled.

Only when his rage dissipated did Trace feel a throbbing in his jaw and the ache in both hands. He unclenched one fist to find the deputy sheriff's badge in his palm.

"Glad I never put up fists against you." Trace turned toward the jail and saw Jerrod Kelly waiting on the boardwalk, supported by a cane. "The shooting scared Holly."

***

After Bradford's body was removed, Trace stood over the puddle of congealing blood, at a loss to his next move. When the floorboards creaked, he looked over his shoulder at Jerrod Kelly. "You're still here."

"I reckon you could use an ally," he said, "since you ran off your deputy."

"The last time we were in this jailhouse together, your brother had me framed for horse theft, and you were watching for an excuse to gun me down."

"I thought we were past that."

"Men don't change," said Trace. "We only hide or reveal who we truly are."

"Don't mistake me for Horne," warned Jerrod.

"All right." Trace moved to stand in front of the map on the wall. "Why would they bother cutting the telegraph wires at all?" Ben had told Trace his part but hadn't gotten to the reason behind it. "Why not just ambush the stage and get away before it's missed?" He took a pin and pressed it into the wood over the stage stop on the map.

"Are you certain it's the strongbox they're after?" Jerrod maneuvered to stand beside him, using the cane for support. "Maybe they're aiming bigger this time." He pointed to the other line that converged on the station—the railroad. "My brothers pulled off a train heist once. They had to use dynamite to get into the safe and ended up blowing apart the express car with it."

"Not Hennessy's style," said Trace. "Could be they're only robbing passengers."

"That's not his style either," said Jerrod, reminding Trace that he and Wyatt once rode together. "Unlike Silas, he liked to keep a job neat, to plan it out, like Rook did."

"Bradford said that Stine used his connections to *uncomplicate* a job," said Trace. "Like making sure the mail wasn't on the stage so the U.S. Marshal didn't get involved."

Jerrod scratched his chin. "If he could manipulate the manifest to reflect nothing in the safe—"

"There'd be no guards," finished Trace. Cutting the wires at the station means they're planning to hold up the train before the stop." From the pin, he traced the tracks northeast with his finger.

"Or," said Jerrod, "they'll do it at the station. What could be easier than walking right up to a sitting bounty." He added, "Bet that station has a handcar."

"If they can unload the safe," said Trace, "they can take and blow it anywhere along the track."

"Any idea when this is going down?"

"Soon," said Trace. "Hennessy met with Stine today."

"You should call up a posse."

Trace shook his head. "Stine's men would be the first to volunteer. I'm on my own."

"There's another option," said Jerrod. "Live to fight another day."

Again, Trace shook his head. With the election coming up, he might not have his authority for much longer. This might be his only opportunity to end the corruption in Prospect. Then there was the matter of Evelyn—or Libby. "Tomorrow could be too late."

"Then you best deputize me," said Jerrod.

"You're in no condition—"

"You need more guns, sheriff," said Jerrod. "I could never face Holly or your family if I let you go alone. You can deny it all you want, but we're practically kin now, Malloy."

"Men don't change," said Trace. "So, I reckon you weren't so bad to begin with."

Jerrod chuckled and shook his head.

"We got to do it according to Hoyle," said Trace, selecting a book off the shelf.

Jerrod leaned his cane against the desk and stood up tall.

Trace said, "Raise your right hand."

17

What will you do after?" Wyatt and Evelyn sat in their saddles overlooking the station from Badger Hill. Below, the stage from Tucson swapped out its team for fresh horses.

"Maybe I'll try out the other side." Wyatt shrugged. "Find some shantytown in need of a lawman." He chuckled at her stunned expression. "Gunwork is gunwork," he said. "Some's legal. Some's not."

"That's not the way Malloy sees it."

"He let you go in Promise."

"You were right," she said. "He regards me only as a wayward woman and expects I'll come to my senses."

A smile played over Wyatt's lips. "Is that what he wanted at The Mare?"

"He tried to persuade me to testify. In exchange, he'll help me to an honest living."

Wyatt raised an eyebrow at her sour tone. "The outlaw life ain't as swell as Silas Kelly made it out to be," he said. "The drifter's path is a lonely one."

"It's just as lonely on the other side," said Evelyn.

A train whistle sounded. "There's our prize." Wyatt pointed to the east where the locomotive billowing black soot ate up track between it and the station.

"What if he shows up?" Evelyn blurted out before she could stop herself.

"He'll be outgunned," said Wyatt. "No mistakes this time, Deveraux. You know your part?" She nodded. "Let's go." He pointed his horse down the incline. Evelyn followed.

They approached at a trot, so the train pulled into the station before they reached it. Four men loitered about the mesquite corral where Wyatt and Evelyn dismounted. To avoid suspicion, they'd posed as passengers and ridden the stage from Tucson.

The Bradford brothers crowded around Wyatt. Evelyn overheard them say they'd received a telegram from Stine before their departure. Word was that Ben had been gunned down that morning while trying to escape.

"We want blood."

"The job comes first," said Wyatt. "You two will get your brothers' shares. We'll deal with Malloy after."

***

While Jerrod went to ready his horse and inform Holly of their departure, Trace paid a visit of his own.

"Is he shot?" Jacob Horne answered his knock, color draining from his face upon finding the sheriff on his doorstep.

"No. But he killed an unarmed man and run off," said Trace. "If you still got kin back east, I suggest you send him back. The man's brothers will be gunning for revenge. All I can do is arrest him." The dentist nodded his understanding. "Easton Stine ought to know where you can find him."

Trace fetched his horse and returned to the jailhouse. His newly sworn-in deputy waited out front. "I stopped by the telegraph office," said Jerrod. They'd discussed sending a warning to the station. "The line went dead sometime after receiving confirmation of the stage's departure."

"The robbery's already underway," said Trace.

"Or will be soon," Jerrod agreed.

***

Train passengers catching the stage to Prospect found the vacancy of four men afforded them seats within the carriage, a luxury compared to balancing atop amongst the mail and luggage. The driver whipped his team and the mud wagon rocked into motion, churning up dust as it gained speed.

The gang loitered about the corral, lounging against the rickety rails, while travelers from the east stretched their legs with a stroll around the station. About the time the stage crested the hill, the conductor called for all to board.

Wyatt led his crew around back of the adobe building. There, one Bradford boosted the other to the roof. Wyatt handed up the cutters and nodded at Evelyn who made her way to the little shack aside the station keeper's abode.

She leaned her shoulder against the doorjamb and stood her rifle along her side. The telegraph officer glanced up then did a double take. "Need to send a message, ma'am?" He continued tapping the key knob, completing the circuit that sent Morse code across the wire. "I'll be right with you as soon as I relay word of the departure to Prospect." Within a few minutes, it was done. The man adjusted his spectacles as he looked her up and down. "Now, what can I do for you?"

"Take a break," she said and spun her rifle to tap the butt against the ceiling, signaling it was time to cut the telegraph wire.

Outside, the Bradford brothers jogged toward the stockcar while Lucas and Jimmy set out to locate the handcar and move it into position. As Evelyn joined Wyatt walking toward the locomotive, nerves struck her like a blast of steam, clouding her vision, engulfing her in heat. Everywhere her eyes darted, she expected to see Malloy. Though she hoped Holly had been successful in persuading the sheriff to abandon his pursuit, the idea that the other woman still wielded such power over his heart crushed her own. "Focus," said Wyatt, sensing her distress even if he couldn't know the cause of it.

Rather than follow the throng up the steps into the passenger cars, he climbed into the engine's cab, pulling his bandana up to conceal his features. The engineer and fireman rounded in surprise when Wyatt announced, "Gentleman, I'm afraid the train is delayed." Gun drawn, he directed them to exit the train on the opposite side passengers were boarding. They all moved toward the express car at the very end. By the time they reached it, the handcar was in position on the section of track parallel.

Wyatt slid open the boxcar door. The safe sat unguarded. "It's empty," the engineer said, exchanging a confused look with the fireman.

"Then there's no reason not to let us take it."

The Bradford brothers came from the stockcar with a length of timber used to load the animals. They bridged the express car and handcar. Wyatt ordered the railroad men to stand against the wall and motioned for Evelyn to guard them. It took all four men plus Wyatt to shove the safe across the floor and over the plank onto the handcar.

After their prize was loaded, Evelyn dashed back to the corral for her and Wyatt's horses. By the time she returned, the trolley was already moving northeast along the rails with two men working the walking beam. Watching them go, Evelyn marveled at how smoothly the job had gone compared to the stagecoach heist. As they left the station behind, the two men not operating the handcar shot their pistols into the air in celebration.

As she came to where Wyatt was waiting, Evelyn glanced up at the passenger windows to see people staring back at her from within, some with confused expressions, others disinterested. She doubted they even knew the train had been held up.

***

Evelyn and Wyatt followed the handcar to where a wagon and mules waited alongside the tracks. Two men sat on the bench seat. Evelyn recognized the driver as one of Stine's employees. Beside him sat Deputy Horne with a black eye and no badge. When Wyatt dismounted, she followed suit. He passed her his reins and moved to help his men. They heaved the safe from trolley to wagon. Jimmy and the Bradford brothers settled down beside it. With a nod from Wyatt, they were underway.

Lucas hopped from the handcar into the sorrel's saddle. "That's my horse," Evelyn complained as he drew the reins from her hand. He directed the mount in an ever-widening circle which she guessed was to disguise their numbers before breaking off to follow the wagon.

Evelyn turned to Wyatt. As he stepped toward her, his expression grim, her hands tightened on the reins to his bay. He reached past her ear and took ahold of her hair at the base of her neck, sweeping it forward over her shoulder. He said, "The one thing folk back there will remember is the woman with the red hair." His hand rested heavy on her shoulder. "Malloy will come," he said. "When he does, you'll have a choice to make."

Wyatt bent over and produced a derringer from his boot. Holding it out to her, he said, "You can kill him and ride his horse to Prospect. Stine will have your reward. Or you can surrender."

Evelyn snatched the gun from his hand and pointed it back at him. "Or I can kill you and take your horse."

His bemused smile held a touch of pride. He turned and mounted the bay, reclaiming the reins with a sharp tug. "Figure out what it is that you really want, Evelyn," he said. "Then go all in."

The image of him galloping away blurred as tears flooded her vision.

***

"There's the stage." Jerrod pointed to the trail of dust five miles or so west of them on the road to Prospect. Trace couldn't make out the coach or team but supposed him correct. They'd saddled up and headed across lots on the most direct course south. After almost ten miles at a brisk pace, they slowed to preserve the horses.

"You all right?" asked Trace. Jerrod was pallid despite the heat and exertion. Dark curls damp with sweat stuck to his face and neck. But he nodded and pressed on. Their path put them in line with the rail as it curved south, and they saw the train sitting at the station, silent and still. Once they got close enough, they saw that some passengers remained on board, but most milled about in the open air. The atmosphere was that of a crisis passed.

While Trace collected statements from the railroad officials, Jerrod showed around wanted posters of known gang members. No one could positively identify any of the men as Hennessy's gang since they'd concealed their faces with bandanas, but all agreed there'd been a woman with long auburn hair among them.

After helping to load the timber taken from the stockcar, Trace instructed the conductor and engineer to get everyone back on board and the train underway.

Trace and Jerrod remounted and cut northeast to intercept the rail line without backtracking. Within a few miles, they could make out the handcar sitting on the tracks. Closer, they discerned a lone figure.

Evelyn sat with one leg dangling over the platform and the other bent so that the toe of her boot was flush with the handcar's edge. She rested her elbow on her knee and leaned back on the opposite hand. Trace rode up to her while Jerrod made a wide circle around the trolley. She lifted the hand from her knee and rotated it palm up, revealing two bullets.

"What are these?" Trace leaned down to take them from her.

"They go to the derringer in my boot." She waited for him to remove the small pistol then sat up, dropping her other leg over the side of the handcar. "I decided to let you take me prisoner after all." The puffiness around her eyes suggested there was more to it than that.

Jerrod reported that it appeared riders had circled back to the handcar after riding off in multiple directions, likely confusing their tracks to mask their numbers and the presence of a wagon for which he'd discovered tracks heading east.

"Where'd they take the safe?"

Evelyn shrugged. "Didn't tell me."

Trace gave her a hard look. "Reckon you were supposed to lead me into an ambush. Only I didn't come alone."

"Believe what you will," she said, turning her head. Trace scrutinized her profile as she blinked away some emotion.

He tossed the derringer to Jerrod then shifted his revolver from his hip to his front, tucking it into his belt close to where his hand gripped the reins. He sidled his buckskin up to the platform so she could climb on behind him.

It was a slow trip back to Prospect. The horses were tired. Jerrod looked pained and fatigued. The events of the day weighed heavy on Trace's mind, none so troublesome as the dilemma of the woman riding double with him. The relief of having Evelyn Deveraux safely back under his protection was negated by the certainty that it wasn't her choice. He wondered whether it was Hennessy or Stine's decree that she be left behind and to what end? Were they ridding themselves of a liability? Or did she serve a more sinister purpose in the two men's plan?

Predicting the designs of women and criminal masterminds was too much for Trace's straightforward way of thinking. He found his logic muddled further as he grappled with the tangle of sensations and emotions prompted by her proximity. She gripped his shoulder for balance only when needed, so maybe it was only his imagination that her fingers toyed with his hair. Whenever he shifted to glimpse her in his peripheral vision, she seemed as lost in her thoughts as he, staring off toward the horizon.

In front of the jailhouse, Trace swept his leg over his mount's neck and slipped from the saddle. He was securing his horse when Holly appeared in the doorway. She rushed to Jerrod who took his wife's head between his hands and kissed her with the urgency of a man returning from war. Trace tore his gaze from the couple to find Evelyn staring down at them, as engrossed in the display of desperate affection as he. The stark wonder on her face made his insides twist. She startled when he touched her arm.

The oil lamp within the jail was lit. A bucket of dark water and pink suds sat by the door, and the floorboards were damp. Holly had made herself busy awaiting their return. Evelyn stepped around the stain, into the cell. As he locked the door, Trace felt a dim sense of relief. Having her in his jail was the next best thing to having her in his bed.

"What happens now?" she asked.

"I make my report." He told her Judge Foster would be in town that Friday.

"So soon? Is he a hanging judge?"

"Give me a reason to advocate leniency and I will."

"Give up Wyatt you mean."

"Your cooperation could save your life."

She glanced at the bloodstain. "It didn't save Ben."

"I can keep you safe."

She finally turned to face him. "So you said." He reckoned that if she wouldn't accept his protection as a lawman, there was no chance she'd consider more.

"Think it over," he said.

Trace stepped outside to find Holly and Jerrod still standing close in quiet conversation. They both fell silent as he emerged from the jailhouse.

"You two can head home," said Trace. "I'll see to the horses. I'm obliged to you both."

Holly looked as if she wanted to say something, but Jerrod drew her away.

When Trace returned, he found Evelyn curled up on the prisoner's cot as if asleep, her boots stowed beneath. He sat behind his desk, intending to start on paperwork. Her form was too tense, his typewriter too silent. He took the flask from the drawer and moved to sit on his own cot. "I'll trade you," he said. "One sip for something true."

For a moment, he thought she would continue to feign sleep. But she sat up and rotated toward him, crossing her ankles in front of her. "I don't know where Wyatt is or where they took the safe."

"That's not what I was going to ask," he said but passed the drink through the bars anyhow. She sipped and held it out to him. Rather than take it back, he lowered his hand to rest upon her foot. "Why did you change your name? What was wrong with Libby?"

She took another swig but found his thumb massaging her arch more compelling than the whisky. "Why did Trace Malloy leave the farm? For adventure? To find his place in the world? I only wanted to escape mine," she said.

"How come?"

"To stay meant I would marry poor, sacrifice my youth to bearing children, many of whom would die. When my face grew haggard, my husband would leave and take with him our son. But he'd leave me our daughter. To feed and clothe her, I'd wash laundry until my hands bled and mend shirts until my eyesight failed, rising each day more weary than the last, until she too left." Trace's hand stilled as he listened. Evelyn wiped the tears from her cheeks, then realizing she hadn't answered his question, said, "After I broke my mother's heart, I couldn't bear to keep the name she'd given me."

Trace lifted his hand and touched her face, brushing away the tear she'd missed. He cupped her jaw, gently urging her toward him. Their noses touched. They shared the same whisky-laden air. Then she pulled back, out of reach. "Kiss me without the bars."

18

His impulse was to throw open the cell door, accept the challenge she'd issued. Trace took the flask and returned it to his desk, giving prudence a chance to weigh in. Time and again, she'd brought him to a line he'd sworn not to cross. He met her more readily each instance. Without a physical barrier, it'd be too easy to forsake his oath, his reputation, his sense. He planted his hands on the desktop and willed rectitude relieve his conflicted heart.

Evelyn hugged her knees to her chest and rested her head against the wall behind her. Her cards were all on the table. Would he answer her call? He moved from his desk to the jailhouse door. She closed her eyes against the sting of rejection.

Trace lowered the drop bar, securing their privacy.

When the cell door clanked open, Evelyn startled. She straightened as he stepped inside, returning her feet to the floor, eyes widening as he moved in front of her. He paused and she waited, fingers clutching the edge of the cot and toes curling against the floorboards.

He nudged her knee with his, twice before she realized his intent. When her thighs parted, he sank to the floor between them. His hands skimmed up her thighs, gripped her hips, and drew her against him. She adjusted her feet, moving them behind his knees, and he felt her toes rest high on his calves, above his boots.

He tore his gaze from parted lips to catch the glimmer in topaz eyes. "Do you know what you want yet, Evelyn?"

She gave a little shake of her head. "Just you," she said.

His kiss stole her breath. Her moan elicited a growl from him. She draped her arms over his shoulders. His banded her back. Her fingers delved into his hair. He gathered hers in his fists. Their kiss deepened and softened as if waxing and waning with the pull of the moon, lasting until each saw stars.

They rested, his breath gusting against her neck, hers stirring his hair. She lowered her hands to his chest. His settled on her hips. Again, she waited, fingers fiddling with a single button on his shirt.

At his nod, her right hand moved down the line, freeing each button, and her left followed, undoing those on the union suit beneath. When she reached his belt, he captured her hands and rising, pulled her to her feet.

He shucked his shirt, peeled long underwear down to hang about his waist. Without her boots, Evelyn's nose was level with his chin. She rose on tiptoes, putting her hands on his biceps for balance, and skimmed her lips along his jaw toward his ear.

Trace clutched her waist, wrestling with the unprecedented predicament of undressing a woman in trousers. She chuckled as his fingers fumbled and teetered as his efforts put her off balance. Patience spent, he spun her back to him and unfastened her belt as easily as his own, one-handed with his other hand splayed over her stomach. The trousers fell from her hips and she stepped out of them, unbuttoning her own shirt while he dispatched his belt, leaving pants to hang on his hips so that a mere shift of clothing would expose him. Evelyn's shirt slipped down her arms. Trace caught it and captured her wrists behind her back, using her sleeve to bind them. He circled round to face her.

She stood before him in loose drawstring drawers and wispy cotton top that seemed too delicate to hold up under men's garments. He forced himself to take his time with each pearl button, ignoring the ache of a swollen groin, watching Evelyn's chest rise and fall with her every breath. Finally, he spread the gauzy curtain, revealing breasts that, untouched by the sun, were milky and soft as cream. Trace cupped one in each hand, then swept his thumbs over each tight nipple.

"Farmer's hands," he muttered when she winced.

"You don't have to apologize for it," she said and something about her words rang familiar.

Trace sat and motioned for Evelyn to step between his knees. A tug on the drawstring was all it took for the garment to flutter down long legs. She trembled as he ran his hands from her calves up the back of her thighs, giving her buttocks a gentle squeeze before framing her hips. He glanced up, found her watching him, nibbling on her lower lip. Not breaking eye contact, he placed one hand at the vee of her thighs, dug fingers into her curls and ground his palm upward. She swayed, regained her balance, then lifted one foot, sliding her arch along the top of his thigh to his hip. Trace rotated his thumb, caressing the wet slit between her legs. When she swayed again, he guided her to sit upon his lap.

With his help, she adjusted her legs to encircle his waist, crossing her ankles at the small of his back and spreading her knees. He released his cock to stretch along the seam of his thighs so that the head just teased her folds. Using his tongue to free her bottom lip from between her teeth, he nipped and sucked while her hands clutched his knee behind her back. When his mouth moved to her breasts, she squirmed on his lap, back bowing to thrust her flesh against his tongue and teeth. Again, he nipped and sucked.

He supported her hips, preventing her from slipping over the side of his thigh, keeping her from impaling herself on his shaft. She moved as much as he would allow, sliding easily in the moisture accumulating between them.

Trace had never held a woman so responsive, hadn't known such a woman existed. He regretted not having a proper bed to sprawl her across.

He didn't want to deny her any longer, could no longer deny himself. "Easy," he whispered as if she were some bangtail he was trying to mount. He reached around her, freed her wrists. She shifted, one hand atop each of his thighs. He gripped his throbbing cock mid-length as her heels dug into his back. When the head breached her opening, she quivered and he cursed. "Easy," he pleaded, working himself deeper. Her breath hitched a little each inch.

Trace stared into eyes like green fire. "You're spectacular."

"Please," she whispered.

He gripped her hips, withdrew, thrust. She bucked, writhing with abandon. He grunted through gritted teeth, white-knuckled as he worked her hips. Evelyn threw back her head and wailed. He shot off inside her as she pulsed around him.

Evelyn melted over him like wax, cheek resting on his shoulder, arms hanging down his back. Trace ran his hands up and down hers, unconsciously returning to some small imperfection along her spine. He circled it with the pad of his finger as the earlier sense of familiarity niggled at his mind. It came to him that the whore he'd bedded in Tucson had a scar in that exact spot. When his hand stilled, Evelyn tensed, and Trace realized it was no coincidence.

He took her shoulders, drew her back until he could see her face, color rapidly fading from her cheeks. She clutched her hands—one over the back of the other—to her chest, tucking her arms close to her torso. She was biting her lip hard enough to draw blood and wouldn't look at him, even when he grasped her chin and tilted her face up toward his. "Evelyn?" He was certain but wanted her admission.

"I wanted to know what it felt like," she said in a halting whisper. Tears spilled down her cheeks.

"What it felt like?" he asked.

"To be loved."

He cupped her face in his hands, stroked her cheeks with his thumbs. Her eyes, wide and wet, finally met his. He kissed her again.

***

They dozed with him lying on his back on the cot and her atop him, knees drawn up against his sides, stirring to make drowsy love by moonlight long after the lamp burnt up all its oil.

At dawn, he shifted out from under her, careful not to wake her, and dressed. The sight of her nude body, marked by his lovemaking, left him dazed. He'd been shocked by her need, awed by her abandon, impassioned by her passion. Loving her had been like riding a storm, one that left its devastation in his heart.

He closed the cell door between them, feeling it was the cruelest thing he'd ever done. He stepped outside to get some air and found the spotted hound curled on the boardwalk.

19

Lack of a breeze combined with stifling heat already had Trace sweating as he trailed the hound to the Kelly home. Jerrod and Tyler sat on chairs on the front porch while little Josiah played at their feet. When the dog collapsed upon the shaded planks, the boy began rearranging his stack of blocks in a line along its heaving side.

"Dog told me you were in town." Trace greeted his brother.

"Came to see how Jerrod was faring," said Tyler. "And that you made it back."

Trace remembered he left the farm in pursuit of Evelyn in the middle of the night without saying farewell. "Reckon you told them the goings-on."

Jerrod nodded. His substitute deputy seemed to have recovered from yesterday's exertion. "You decide your course, sheriff?"

Trace had considered Evelyn's predicament on the walk over. "Miss Deveraux was intended to be a scapegoat," he said. "Judge Foster ought to understand Hennessy led her astray as part of his plan. Maybe he'll only charge her time served."

"Trust you won't make it too uncomfortable for her."

Trace ignored the comment. "Aimee inside?" Tyler nodded.

He opened the door and was met with the heat of a kitchen stove. "Leave that open, will you, Trace?" called Beth. Wisps of hair escaped her bun to float about her face as she kneaded dough at the table. Aimee rose from in front of the oven, steaming pans of bread in each mitted hand. As she moved aside, Holly slid in a new batch and shut the cast iron door. She greeted him brightly, cheeks made extra rosy by the heat. Trace asked to speak with Aimee, and she joined him in the parlor area, swiping a sleeve across her brow. She faced him, curiosity in gray eyes.

"Jerrod told you about the incident yesterday, about Casey Horne being in cahoots with Wyatt Hennessy and company?"

She nodded. "I'm so sorry, Trace."

"Not as sorry as I am," said Trace. "I recommended him to you." He searched her face for some indication of how she was handling the news, ever worried that the hardships of being a widow and mother would bring back the weak constitution of her childhood.

But she smiled and said, "Luckily my heart doesn't succumb upon recommendation alone."

He felt more concerned than relieved. "You deserve more."

"I have more than I ever dared to hope." She nodded toward the porch where her son's efforts to kiss the hound on the nose were thwarted by the canine licking his face instead. "He isn't his father any more than Josiah was his father."

"I've treated him unjustly," acknowledged Trace.

"He's still young enough to forgive and forget it," she said, shrugging off his apology. "What becomes of Miss Deveraux?"

Trace noted that conversation in the kitchen had fallen to the level of whispers, though Holly and Beth were careful to keep their eyes on their baking. "I aim to help her, if I can."

"I like her," said Aimee. "We all do." She kissed his cheek and returned to the others. Before he left, Holly invited him to supper that evening.

Outside, Trace ruffled the blond locks so like his mother's. The boy looked up, blinked blue eyes, then went back to stacking blocks. And for the first time, Trace pitied him all he had yet to learn—of his father, of the world, of the reputation tied to his name that would be his burden to change.

Jerrod stood to hand him something. "Resigning already?" Trace tucked the badge into his vest pocket.

"You need reinforcements, you know where to find me."

***

Trace stopped by the boarding house. The heat was making him itch, so he decided to wash and change clothes. As he dumped the basin of water, it occurred to him that Evelyn too might enjoy the opportunity to freshen up. He tucked the basin and a new washrag under his arm and started for the jailhouse.

The solution he devised on his earlier walk took on the form of a plan. If Judge Foster dismissed the case against her, Trace was ready to make Evelyn an offer. He didn't even want to wait for the election, unwilling to give up what he'd found last night to appease convention. His constituents would just have to accept their sheriff's choice of wife. Evelyn could stay at the farm until he secured them better lodging than the boarding house.

Trace's stride slowed when he spotted two men standing outside the jailhouse. One was Easton Stine. It took him a few more steps to recognize the other.

"Judge Foster," said Trace. "I didn't expect you in town this early."

"News of the railroad holdup reached me in Maricopa," said the judge. "I heard that you made an arrest, a woman."

"Miss Deveraux has ties to the Hennessy gang, but she isn't a hardened criminal." Trace glanced at Stine. "I suspect the men who masterminded the robbery intended her to get caught."

"A patsy?" said Foster. "Has she informed on her confederates?"

"I reckon she might be more cooperative if she knew she wasn't facing charges," said Trace.

"Perhaps she'll open up in a more comfortable setting." Stine chimed in before Trace could advocate Evelyn's release. "Our good sheriff's reputation isn't one of a forgiving man."

Trace glowered at the town marshal. "Hennessy has a secret partner, a man with connections. My last witness was assassinated before—"

"In your jailhouse by your deputy," said Stine. "Whom, I might add, got away."

Foster lifted a hand to quell the argument. "Let Marshal Stine take custody of the prisoner. I'll hear the case tomorrow morning." Anticipating Trace's protest, he said, "Though I appreciate your perspective, sheriff, in my experience, a prisoner is more likely to give up his accomplices when facing punishment. I expect this holds true in the case of a woman."

Trace reluctantly offered to walk the prisoner over, but Stine said, "I might as well collect her now since I'm here." For Trace's ears only, he added, "Wouldn't want her to escape again."

Trace lowered his voice. "If she doesn't make it to court tomorrow, Foster will know your hands are dirty."

"She'll make it to court." Stine smiled.

Trace unlocked the door and moved through first, using his body to block the others' view. Relieved to find Evelyn awake and dressed, he realized the two men must have knocked, rousing her. He set the items he was carrying on his cot and stepped up to the bars. "This is Judge Foster. He's decided that—"

"I'll be taking care of you tonight." The town marshal crowded alongside the sheriff, squaring his shoulders and sticking out his chest though he couldn't match Trace's height or breadth. Evelyn's wary gaze drifted between them.

Trace noticed her hands shook when he fastened the manacles around her wrists. He wished to reassure her, but the hovering businessman gave them no opportunity for so much as a quiet word. He feared anything more than an impartial touch would be detected by shrewd eyes and didn't have the talent for communicating tender feelings with a mere look.

Stine held out his hand for the key, then took Evelyn's elbow. She walked through the door and turned the corner, passing out of his sight, his protection, his future.

Left alone in his jail, Trace picked the basin back up and hurled it. It hit the safe and shattered, shards ricocheting to all corners of the room.

***

As Evelyn followed Stine, his shorter stride forced her to shuffle. Though the stares from townsfolk were similar to those she'd received the afternoon Trace arrested her, she felt like a prisoner for the first time. Before, capture had been a choice, part of a larger plan. Now, the man who would decide her fate trailed her like a shadow.

Business at The Old Mare was slow during the daylight hours. Stine led Evelyn and the judge upstairs to his office. As Foster made himself comfortable, pulling up a chair to the desk and helping himself to the town marshal's bourbon, Stine ushered her through the French doors.

A zinc tub had been lugged upstairs and situated at the foot of the four-poster. Evelyn could only guess how many buckets had been required to fill it. As Stine removed the manacles, he explained the silk wrapper, hairbrush, and assortment of soaps and perfumes atop the vanity were for her use. He told her to ring the bell should she have need of anything, that otherwise, he would ensure she was not disturbed. He left, closing the doors between them. She listened to his footsteps moving to join the judge and heard the rumble of male voices.

Evelyn tested the water, discovering it still hot, brushed out her hair, and sampled the toiletries, finding them all too prominent for her liking. As the conversation droned on, she decided a bath would calm her nerves and ease the soreness between her thighs. She thought of Trace as she unfastened her belt and again when she loosened the strings on her undergarments.

She sank into the bath and was still there when footfalls passed the double doors. She relaxed when the office door opened and closed, leaning her head back against the metal rim, allowing her eyelids to drift shut. When her thoughts turned toward the morrow, she comforted herself with memories of her night with the sheriff. Trace Malloy had surprised her. As a lover, the lawman was both generous and demanding, powerful yet gentle, and more adventurous than his straight-shooting constitution suggested.

She knew from her previous occupation that intimacy was often nothing more than a hunger that once satisfied, built again. But sometimes, a man's appetites offered insight into his true nature, at odds with the face he showed to the world. She found Malloy exactly who he presented himself to be and loved him the more for it. But there was also more to him, something of himself that he saved for those he loved and trusted, that he'd shared with her. Their lovemaking ranged from lazy to frenzied as they made the most of the dark hours before inevitable dawn, as if it were all the time they would have.

Sorrow speared her recollection before she assured herself that, like her, he would find just one night inadequate. He would come for her. Unless he deemed his duty above himself as many men claimed but few practiced. The idea that he might be one of those few made her worry for him as much as herself. Evelyn also knew that the things that filled men were oft times the same things that emptied them.

Something—a current of air colder than her doubts—alerted her, and she opened her eyes to see Stine staring down at her. She resisted the impulse to cover herself, hoping defiance would spoil his enjoyment of her nakedness.

"I thought you'd be done by now," he said, and Evelyn realized the water had turned quite cool. "I'm having an early supper fixed for you." Though her stomach growled, she couldn't bring herself to thank him.

He nudged the pile of clothing she'd left on the floor with the toe of his boot. "About tomorrow," he said. "All you really must do is decide what to wear." He moved to the wardrobe in the corner, opened the door, and removed a fine dress, hooking its hanger on the adjacent coat rack. "Should you wear it to your trial, I will know you've accepted my offer," he said. "And Judge Foster will know to find you innocent."

In spite of herself, Evelyn drew her knees up to her chest and hunched behind them. "And if I don't?"

"Then you will be found guilty and sent to Yuma Prison," he said. "Enjoy your bath and your meal. I hope you don't decide they will be your last."

There was a tap on the door. At Stine's acknowledgment, a young woman entered with the meal. When she turned to leave, Evelyn said, "Can she stay? I may need assistance."

"I'm sure you can manage," said Stine. "I'll be up all night, so you can rest assured, no one will intrude upon your reflection." His eyes wandered over her bare limbs once more. "If the sheriff comes calling, I'll let him know you're tucked safely in my bed." He left and Evelyn heard the door lock.

She climbed out of the water, shivering as she dressed in the cotton top and drawers. She'd lost her appetite for the generous meal. It grew cold as she paced. She refused to touch the grand bed or inspect the exquisite dress. Weary, she sat at the vanity and folded her arms on its surface to cushion her head.

20

Promise was a ghost town once more. Trace sensed it as soon as he started down the main drag. He decided he didn't like Evelyn's odds. Though he'd never heard of Foster sentencing a woman to death, the judge had sent enough to Yuma. If Evelyn wouldn't give up Hennessy, it was up to Trace to find him. Promise was his only viable lead. He had to come, if only to confirm his doubts.

He'd left the jailhouse at once, had gone to the telegraph office and sent messages to every station within a hundred miles. *Trial tomorrow. Prospect. She'll answer for your crimes. Turn yourself in coward.* If Hennessy had any decency, any pride, maybe he would heed.

Trace wasn't going to wait around. He needed action. Promise might be a futile errand but at least he wasn't idle. He explored the abandoned buildings, devoid of clues, while his horse recuperated for the return journey.

During the ride back to Prospect, he considered his options and wondered if he could live with either. He could forfeit his badge and the town to Stine, allow the corruption he'd worked to oust to take root once more. Or he could abandon another good woman for the sake of his principles.

His first stop was The Old Mare. He waded through the crowd and was met at the base of the stairs by Easton Stine.

"Where's Foster staying?" Trace decided to tell the judge that the town marshal was in league with outlaws. Damn the proof.

"The judge is... retired for the night," said Stine, looking toward one of the whores' rooms above them.

"And Miss Deveraux?"

"Weighing her options in luxury like she's never known before." Trace's gaze went to Stine's office where two of his police stood guard outside the door. "I promised her she wouldn't be disturbed."

"Will you give her a message?"

"Of course." From the inside pocket of his frock coat, Stine produced a pad of paper and an expensive-looking pen. He held them as if prepared to take dictation.

Trace was tempted to snatch the materials out of the man's hands but reckoned Stine would read the note anyhow. "Hennessy is gone," he began, then realized he had neither wit nor words to express all he wanted to say to her. His plain speech was inadequate. Stine waited with pen poised. "Please consider your own best interests," he concluded, hoping she counted him among them.

Stine closed his notepad with a flourish. "Exactly the advice I gave her," he said. Trace wanted to punch him.

By the time he opened the jailhouse door, it was dark inside. His boots crunched on broken porcelain. He found the lamp then remembered it was out of oil. He rummaged through the desk drawers until he felt a candle. Then struck a match. The meager light gave shape to a man reclined on the cot outside the cell.

"Son of a bitch." Trace dropped the match and it went out. He struck another as the man sat up. "You've got a lot of nerve."

"I could say the same about you," said Wyatt Hennessy.

Trace managed to light the candle. "Have you come to turn yourself in?" He searched for and found the oil can.

"What good would that do?"

"Justice would prevail."

Wyatt snorted. "Bribes will prevail. Stine owns the judge, owns the entire town but for you."

Trace got the lamp refilled and lit, then snuffed out the candle. "Then why'd you come?"

"Stine keeps altering our arrangement. He altered it one time too far by demanding Deveraux as part of his share."

"He can't have what's yours?"

"If she were mine, I wouldn't have sent her to you." Trace didn't know how to respond to that. "Stine's accustomed to getting what he wants, and he has money to buy the means. There isn't much an honorable sheriff can do," said Wyatt. "But a common cowboy or dare I presume, a man in love?" He raised his eyebrows. "I'm here to offer my assistance."

"So are we." Another voice joined the conversation as Jerrod and Tyler stepped into the jailhouse. "He doesn't own the whole town," Jerrod told Wyatt.

Tyler said, "What is the plan, exactly?"

Trace listened to the scheme, too stunned to interject anything helpful. Once it was all laid out, the three men awaited his response. "If I leave town, there'll be no one to contest Stine."

"I'll take up the badge," said Jerrod.

Wyatt said, "I'll be his deputy."

Before Trace found his voice, there came a pounding on the jailhouse door. "Tyler Malloy. Jerrod Kelly. You were supposed to bring him half an hour ago," Beth scolded through it. "Supper's gone cold."

"I could use a bite," said Wyatt.

Tyler opened the door. "You sound like a mama already," he said, earning a glower though his wife's cheeks went pink.

The four men trailed Beth like troublesome boys, back to the Kelly home. Trace put his hand on Tyler's shoulder and spoke into his ear. "Is Beth?"

A grin split the younger man's face. "She thinks it's too early to share the news. I'm ready to shout it to the whole town."

Trace gave his brother a congratulatory slap on the back. Behind them, Jerrod and Wyatt were still discussing their uncharacteristic collaboration.

***

The dining room table wasn't big enough for all, so Trace and Wyatt sat in the parlor chairs with plates balanced on their knees while the others clustered around the spread.

Little Josiah squirmed off his mother's lap halfway through the meal to play beneath the table, crawling around legs and chairs, stealing morsels for the hound that kept him company.

Hennessy chuckled. "Who does the lad belong to?" he asked. "Josiah is it?"

"My sister, Aimee." Trace felt a twinge of guilt, realizing this reunion might be the last he'd attend for some time, that he'd likely miss the birth of his brother's first child. His career had taken priority during the last couple years. Now, to see to his own happiness, he'd miss out on theirs. He hoped that Jerrod would have better success ousting Stine, which led him to consider the gunfighter's choice of deputy.

If he believed Hennessy was looking out for Evelyn by leaving her behind to be arrested, it would seem the outlaw had a decent streak. Trace was skeptical, but Jerrod would know better how deep that redeeming grain might run. Trace realized he'd have to trust Kelly's judgement.

Later, as Beth cleared the table and Holly made coffee, Aimee collected their plates. "Thank you, Miss Malloy," said Wyatt.

"It's Mrs. Wyland," she said.

"My apologies."

Once the table was cleared, the men sat around it, enjoying coffee before it was time to put their plan into action. The child was put to bed, so Aimee sat in the parlor with a book. Holly refilled their mugs and when Jerrod stepped out to use the privy, took a seat beside Trace. Seeing she wanted a word with the sheriff, Tyler excused himself to "tuck Beth in," and Wyatt moved to the adjacent room.

Trace thought she might be worried for Jerrod's safety. Instead, she said, "It still hurts that I wasn't enough for you when I would have done anything for you." She held up a hand to stop his response. "I know Evelyn is the one because of what you're willing to give up." She smiled though she blinked to hold back tears.

"I don't even know who I am if not sheriff," he said.

"You're more than your badge, Trace," she said. "Though maybe you need to give it up to be able to see that. Take this chance, so that I don't have to worry for you, so that I can be free of you." He looked up to see Jerrod in the doorway, stood and moved away so that his once-rival could comfort his once-love.

In the parlor, he found Wyatt watching his sister read. Without looking up, she said, "Did you know my husband, Mr. Hennessy?"

"Only by reputation."

She fixed gray eyes on him and lifted her chin. "Then you didn't know him at all."

"No, ma'am," he said. "I suppose not."

She nodded and satisfied, went back to her reading. Wyatt was still watching her when Trace moved beside him. "Finish your coffee," he grumbled. "It's time we got a move on."

21

Evelyn awoke periodically during the night and listened to the din of the busy saloon or the knocking of a bedframe in an adjacent room before readjusting her head atop her arms and drifting off again. Occasionally, she stared at the line of light at the base of the French doors, wondering if the footsteps beyond were real or imagined.

When she awoke again to quiet, she realized it must be near dawn. She stretched, dressed, and brushed her hair in the dark, then sat awaiting the sun and her trial.

As gray light gradually filled the room, she watched her reflection take shape in the mirror. First, it revealed her form, much the same as it had been since womanhood, then the contours that distinguished her face. When sunrise breached the window sill, Evelyn saw herself imbued with color. Her hair blazed red, her eyes shone topaz, and her freckled complexion took on the hue of a ripe peach.

But it wasn't her beauty that satisfied her. From a girl fleeing her origins, wishing for rescue, she'd finally transformed. She stared into the eyes of a woman as courageous as any man, who'd sought an identity of her own making and was prepared to accept the fate that went with it.

When the knock came, Evelyn stood. And realized Easton Stine had granted her every option, so confident was he that she would choose the dress and him. There was a window through which she might have fled and the tub of cold water which offered a different form of escape. Evelyn also realized she had considered no option but the one she'd chosen.

The door opened. Stine stood looking her up and down in silence before shaking his head. Dryly, he said, "You are a sight to behold, Miss Deveraux." He locked her wrists together once more. "It's a shame Malloy isn't here to see it."

The Old Mare had served as Prospect's courtroom even when Cooper was judge. The gaming tables were pushed to the perimeter of the room, stacked face-to-face, with the chairs arranged in rows before the mahogany bar. Each was claimed and the surplus of men and women stood crowding the floor behind. At the top of the stairs, Evelyn took a moment to scan the spectators' faces, hoping Stine was wrong. She saw only strangers.

At her jailor's side, she descended, her boots knocking each step the only sound. She was directed to face the bar behind which Judge Foster stood elevated, a paragon of authority, above the assemblage. He scrutinized Evelyn, taking in the cotton shirt and trousers, before exchanging a nod with the town marshal.

"Miss Deveraux," he said, projecting his words out over the crowd. "I have read the statements of several eyewitnesses who identified you as party to the holdup of the Southern Pacific train at Badger Hill Station Tuesday last, during which the safe containing $80,000 in gold and silver was stolen from the express car." Foster paused, giving his audience a moment to absorb the information. "Since you have refused to reveal the names of your confederates or the location of the stolen bullion, you will bear full punishment for this transgression." He paused again as a murmur of anticipation spread through the room. "I hereby sentence you to serve ten years in Yuma Prison." He reached for his gavel and raised his voice, rushing to finish before the crowd's enthusiasm overpowered his verdict. "Marshal Stine will escort you via horseback to Maricopa Station, where the train will arrive to carry you to serve out your term." He slammed the wooden hammer down upon the bar. "Court is adjourned."

Stine took Evelyn's elbow and directed her outside to where the horses were already waiting. She had to stretch to reach the horn with bound hands but hauled herself up into the saddle without assistance. As spectators began to pour through the batwing doors, a familiar well-dressed brunette slipped out with them. Evelyn had missed Mrs. Jerrod Kelly among the audience.

Holly's eyes met hers, but the clear sky-blue gaze conveyed nothing. Evelyn watched her move a short distance down the boardwalk before climbing atop a wagon. Her figure joined two others—one taller and one shorter—upon the bench seat. Evelyn thought they might be Beth and Aimee.

Her ride was tethered to another belonging to one of four armed men. When Stine led them down Main Street, past the jail, Evelyn hoped she might yet see Trace one last time. But the jailhouse door was shut. She had no way of knowing if he was even inside. As they turned westward, out of Prospect, the guard in front of Evelyn took the lead and Stine fell back to ride beside her. He said, "It would seem the gallant sheriff isn't one for goodbyes."

The journey to Maricopa was nearly twenty miles and would take much of the day. Evelyn lost herself in the landscape which had a way of looking the same. Occasionally, a feature would arrest her attention. They crossed an arroyo that could have been the very one from which Trace rescued her. She scanned a distant outcropping of rocks but couldn't pick out the cave where they'd taken shelter. For a time, they traveled along the Gila River but turned northwest before she could catch sight of the Malloy farmhouse or even the tree on the ridge above it.

An old wagon road led them past a group of abandoned sod houses imbedded in a hillside. Evelyn's gaze stuck with one of the dilapidated structures, and she envisioned a bent old woman outside of it, watching for her return.

After that, Evelyn paid little attention to their progress. She didn't notice the sun traveling across the sky, lost count of how many times Stine swabbed his brow and the back of his neck with his handkerchief.

Finally, their destination came into view. To Evelyn, Maricopa appeared just another boomtown. They might have circled and come back to Prospect, so similar were the two settlements in size and layout, except for the railway, converging from the south. The train that would take her to Yuma already sat at the station.

There were no passenger cars coupled to the locomotive. It was hauling only livestock and goods. Stine spoke to the engineer who directed them to a boxcar segregated into animal stalls and pens. Evelyn was hoisted inside.

The front part of the car was littered with straw which one of the guards swept aside to reveal tie-down points on the floor.

Stine ordered her to kneel. The man ran a section of chain through one of the iron loops and around her handcuffs, connecting the links with a padlock. He handed the key to Stine who stood over her, shaking his head. "What a waste," he said.

When he continued to stand there, she lifted her chin. "I hope you're not expecting me to confess my regrets," she said. "Because I have none."

"You will, inevitably," he said. "Though it would have been some consolation to see you shed that first tear." He paused as if waiting for her to oblige. "I almost forgot. Malloy left you a message." He fished a notepad out of his coat's inner pocket and rifled through the pages. "Please consider your own best interests," he quoted. He turned the page as if looking for more, shrugged, and flipped the booklet closed.

Evelyn's shoulders slumped. She turned her head so he couldn't read the disappointment in her eyes. "His advice might serve you yet. I may come visit you, see if prison warms you to my regard," he said. "When I'm sheriff, I could appeal to the governor for your pardon. That is, if your case still compels me."

The door slid shut after him, and a few minutes later, the train began to move. It was dim inside but not dark. Through the cracks in the railcar's sides, the painted desert was a blur. Evelyn sat with her legs folded beneath her, shackled hands in her lap. The metal was cold, the tears that rained down upon her skin warm. She couldn't tell if it was her own trembling or the vibrations of the train that made the chains clink. She closed her eyes. Then jerked when a warm tongue lapped at her salty cheeks.

"What are you doing here?" she asked the spotted dog.

"He came to say goodbye."

22

Evelyn had seen him so often in her memories throughout the day that she didn't quite trust the stowaway emerging from one of the stalls was truly Trace, even when he knelt in front of her very eyes. She raised her hands to touch him. With a clank, the chain went taut, and she let them fall back to her lap. He covered both her hands with one of his, warm and real.

"I looked for you at the trial," she said.

"I had arrangements to make." His own best interests to see to, thought Evelyn. "I'm sorry."

Staring into his sympathy-softened golden eyes caused her own to fill. She wanted so much more than his apology. Her gaze fell to his chest. "Where's your star?"

"I've decided to follow my own sense of right." Her eyes snapped back to his. "Let my heart guide me," he said.

Hope hurt. Evelyn had forgotten the desperate press of it, expanding against the ribcage, squeezing the lungs, wringing the heart. She wondered if he felt it too.

Shadows swarmed about them. It was growing dark inside the railcar. Evelyn realized the sun was setting on the outside world. "Is the train slowing down?"

"Our stop is coming up." He raised his other hand to cup her jaw. "Please say you'll come with me."

"Where?" She breathed the question.

"Wherever the wind takes us." Trace could no longer see her face in front of his, couldn't read her eyes to know whether she understood. "Evelyn?"

"Yes." She paused, then repeated, "Yes."

He realized it was her answer. His lips found hers in the dark. He rose to his knees, pulled her body against his, and deepened the kiss.

The door slid open. The fading light of a low sun flooded the car and backlit a man Evelyn thought she recognized as Jerrod Kelly. "There will be time for that later," he said, handing something to Trace. When the manacles fell away, she realized it must have been a key. Trace stood and pulled her to her feet.

The spotted dog led the way off the train. A sliver of sun on the horizon illuminated the silhouettes of men and horses dwarfed by the water tower beyond. Evelyn wondered if the locomotive really needed filling or if it was only meant to look that way from distant Maricopa. Nearer the structure, she saw that Tyler Malloy waited on horseback with her sorrel and Trace's buckskin saddled and ready.

Jerrod waved to another rider up by the engine. Wyatt Hennessy signaled the engineer to be on his way then rode back to join the group as the locomotive chugged into motion.

Rather than say their goodbyes at the edge of the tracks, they rode a short distance together, to where a wagon waited. One of the figures hopped up from her seat to wave, curls bouncing off her shoulders.

Holly was the first to embrace Evelyn, as easily as if they were sisters. While she received the women's warm wishes, Tyler helped Trace transfer stocked saddlebags from the back of the wagon to their horses. Then Trace hoisted the hound up into the cart. It bounded to the front to join the sleeping boy curled up on blankets.

"Don't wake him," he told Aimee. "Tell him to mind his ma and take good care of that mutt."

While Trace shared a hug with his brother and handshake with Jerrod, Wyatt wished Evelyn good luck. "Told you we aren't all the same," he said.

Finally, Trace and Wyatt shook hands. "I'm serious, Hennessy," said Trace. "Stay away from my sister." Wyatt only grinned.

THE END

MORGAN LEE WYLIE lives in Idaho with her husband, daughter, dogs, and horses. She and her husband are expecting their second child New Year's Day 2021.

To learn more about Morgan, her writing process, and current projects, please follow her on Instagram @morganleewylie.

To receive an email when Morgan's next book is released, please join her mailing list at https://morganleewylie.com/signup.

Did you enjoy this book?

Please leave a review.

ALSO BY MORGAN LEE WYLIE

UNSCRUPULOUS

(A Romantic Western Adventure Novel)

He's a gunfighter with a bad reputation.
She's the sheriff's wife he's sent to rescue.
A raw and gritty tale of redemption, second chances, and forbidden love.

www.ingramcontent.com/pod-product-compliance
Lightning Source LLC
Chambersburg PA
CBHW021158110726
47900CB00002B/638

* 9 7 8 1 7 3 2 4 8 5 3 2 7 *